A TREASURY OF
Magical Stories

Written by
Derek Hall, Alison Morris and Louisa Somerville

PARRAGON

Illustrated by
Jeremy Bays, Natalie Bould, Lynn Breeze, Anna Cattermole,
Maureen Galvani, Mary Hall, Virginia Margerison, Paula Martyr, Julia Oliver,
Martin Orme, Sara Silcock, Gillian Toft, Kerry Vaughan, Jenny Williams,
Kirsty Wilson

Designed by Louise Millar

First published in 1998 by
PARRAGON
13 Whiteladies Road
Clifton
Bristol BS8 1PB

Copyright © 1998 Parragon

Created and produced for Parragon by
Linda Watters Book Packagin
8 Trent Close
Shenley
Herts WD7 9HX

ISBN 0-75252-840-8

Printed in Italy

A TREASURY OF
Magical Stories

Contents

The Dragon Who Was Scared of Flying

Once upon a time, in a land far away, there lived a dragon named Dennis. He lived in a cave high up in the mountains. All his friends lived in caves nearby, and his own brothers and sisters lived right next door. Now you would think that Dennis would have been a very happy dragon, surrounded by his friends and family, wouldn't you? Well, I'm sorry to say that Dennis was, in fact, a very unhappy and lonely dragon.

The reason for this was that Dennis was scared of flying. Every day his friends would set off to have adventures, leaving poor Dennis behind on his own. Dennis would stare out of his cave at the departing dragons. How he wished he could join them!

After they had gone, he would stand on the ledge outside his cave, trying to build up the courage to fly. But as soon as he looked over the edge, he felt all giddy and had to step back. Then he would crawl back into his cave defeated and spend the rest of the day counting stalagtites on the ceiling or rearranging his collection of bat bones.

Every evening, the other dragons would return with amazing tales of what they had been up to that day. "I rescued a damsel in distress," one would say.

"I fought the wicked one-eyed giant and won," boasted another.

"I helped light the fire for a witch's cauldron," announced a third.

"What have you been up to?" Dennis's sister Doreen used to ask him.

"Oh... um... this and that," Dennis would reply mournfully, looking down at his scaly toes. Then Doreen would lead him out of the cave and try to teach him to fly. Dennis would take a running jump and flap his wings furiously but his feet would stay firmly on the ground. Then the other dragons would laugh so much that, in the end, he always gave up.

One day, Dennis could stand it no longer. The other dragons flew off as usual to find adventure but Dennis, instead of retreating into his cave, set off down the mountain side. It was very tiring having to walk. Dennis had never really been further than from his cave to the ledge and back, and soon he was puffing and panting. He was about to rest at the side of the path when his eye was caught by something colourful in the distance. Down in the valley he could make out some brightly coloured tents, and now he could hear the faint strains of music drifting up to him. "I'd better take a closer look," thought Dennis. "Maybe I can have an adventure, like the other dragons!" He got so excited at the thought of his very own adventure that he started to run. Then he got all out of breath and had to stop altogether for a while.

At last Dennis reached the tents and found himself in a world more exotic than he could ever have imagined. He was surrounded by strange, four-legged creatures, such as he had never seen before. There was a yellow creature that roared and another one with stripes and fierce teeth. There were also quite a few hairy creatures with long tails. These ones were dressed up to look like boys and girls. Can you guess what all these creatures were? Of course, Dennis had never seen a lion or a tiger or a chimpanzee before. He thought they were very peculiar! The animals thought Dennis was very odd, too. They stood in a circle around him. "How strange," snarled the lion. "A slimy thing with wings!"

"It doesn't look very fit!" growled the tiger, flexing his claws.

"Look at its funny, knobbly tail," giggled the chimpanzees.

Dennis began to feel unhappy and unwanted again, but at that moment he heard a friendly voice saying, "Hello, there! Welcome to Chippy's Circus. I'm Claude the clown. How do you do?"

Dennis turned round. Now he felt really confused, for standing behind him was a man with the unhappiest face Dennis had ever seen. He had great sad eyes and a mouth that was turned down so far that it seemed to touch his chin. Yet he spoke so cheerfully!

"I'm Dennis the dragon," said Dennis.

"A dragon, eh?" said Claude. "Well, we've never had a dragon in the circus before. Might be quite a crowd puller! Would you like to join the circus?" he asked.

"Oh, yes please," cried Dennis.

"Very well," said Claude. "I'm sure you're very talented," he added.

So Dennis joined the circus and was happy for the first time in his life. The other animals became quite friendly now that they knew what he was. Claude taught Dennis to ride the unicycle and to do acrobatic tricks. He also learned how to dive into a bucket of water. He didn't mind that a bit because his slimy skin was quite waterproof! Now, as you know, dragons are particularly

10

good at breathing fire, so Dennis soon became the circus's champion fire-eater. Folk would come from far and near to see Dennis shooting flames high into the dark roof of the big top.

One evening Dennis had just finished his fire-eating act. He was eating an icecream to cool his hot throat and watching Carlotta, the tight-rope walker. She was pirouetting high up on the rope as usual. Then all at once she lost her footing and Dennis saw to his horror that she was going to fall. He dropped his icecream and, without thinking, flapped his wings furiously. As Carlotta fell, Dennis found himself flying up towards her. He caught her gently on his back and flew down to the ground with her clinging on tightly. The crowd roared and burst into applause. They obviously thought it was all part of the act.

"Thank you, Dennis," whispered Carlotta in Dennis's ear. "You saved my life."

Dennis was overjoyed. Not only had he saved Carlotta's life, he had also learned to fly. And he said with a grin, "I do declare that flying is actually rather fun."

The Naughty Broom

"Goodness me, what a lot of dirt and dust there is all over this kitchen floor," said the maid. She was a very house-proud maid, and didn't like dirt and dust on her floor one little bit. Out came the broom from its place in the cupboard in the corner, and soon the maid was busily sweeping the floor and brushing all the dirt and dust into a big dustpan.

Unfortunately, this kitchen also had elves living in it. They were too tiny to see, of course, but if you upset them they could be very mischievous indeed. As the broom worked away, it swept into one dark corner where the elves were having a party. Suddenly the king elf was swept away from their little table and into the dustpan! The next thing he knew he was being thrown, with all the other rubbish, on to the rubbish tip.

Coughing and spluttering with rage, the king elf finally climbed out from under all the rubbish in the rubbish tip and stood on top of it. He picked the dirt and dust out of his ears and nose, pulled a fish bone from out of his trousers and tried to look as king-like as he could, having just been thrown on to a rubbish tip. "Who did this?" he squeaked at the top of his voice. "I'll make someone very, very sorry indeed," he vowed.

Eventually he made his way back to the house, and into the kitchen again. The other elves looked at the king elf and did their best not to laugh. For the king elf was still looking very dirty and untidy, and still had bits of rubbish stuck all over him. But the other elves knew better than to laugh at the king, because he was likely to cast a bad spell on them if they did.

"It was the broom that did it," chorused all the other elves.

"Right," said the king elf, "then I'm going to cast a bad spell on the broom."

The broom was by now back in its cupboard. The king elf marched over to the cupboard and jumped in through the keyhole. The king elf pointed to the broom and said,

"Bubble, bubble, gubble, gubble,

Go and cause a lot of trouble!"

And with that the broom suddenly stood to attention, its bristles quivering. It was night time now and everyone in the house was asleep. The broom opened its cupboard door and sprang into the kitchen. It then unlocked the kitchen door and went outside. Straight to the rubbish tip it went, and with a flick of its bristles, swept a huge pile of rubbish back into the kitchen. Tin cans, dirt, dust, chicken bones and goodness knows what else all got swept on to the kitchen floor. The broom then closed the kitchen door, took itself back to its cupboard and all was quiet until morning.

When the maid came down into the kitchen, she couldn't believe her eyes. "Who has made this awful mess?" she said. "If I find out it was those cats . . ." she threatened. She took the broom from the cupboard and swept all the rubbish back outside again.

The next night, the same thing happened. Once it was quiet and everyone in the house was asleep, out of its cupboard came the broom, and into the house came all the rubbish again, swept there as before by the naughty broom. This time, there were fish heads, old bottles and all the soot from the fireplaces.

Well, the maid was speechless. After clearing up again, she got the gardener to burn all the rubbish from the rubbish tip, so that nothing else could be brought in – although she still had no idea how it had happened.

That very night, the naughty broom decided it would make a mess in a different way. So instead of sweeping in rubbish from outside, the broom flew up to the shelves and knocked all the jars to the ground. With a crash they fell to the floor, one after another, and spread their contents everywhere.

"Stop this AT ONCE!" demanded a voice suddenly.

The broom stopped its mischief.

"What do you think you are doing?" said the voice again. The voice had come from a very stern-looking fairy who was now standing on the draining board, with her hands on her hips. What the broom did not know was that one of the bottles it had knocked down contained a good fairy, imprisoned by the elves. Now she was at last free, the spell was broken and it was her turn to cast a spell.

16

"Broom, broom, sweep this floor,
Make it cleaner than ever before.
Find the elves that cast your spell,
And sweep them off into the well," she chanted.

The broom went to work. It seemed to sweep so fast that its bristles just became a blur. Into this corner it went, then into that, and into every nook and cranny it swept. Every bit of dirt and dust, and all the broken bottles, were swept into the dustpan and then out of the house. Then it came back and swept all the elves down into the well where they couldn't do any more mischief.

In the morning, the maid came down to find a spotlessly clean kitchen. She was puzzled to find some of the jars missing, but between you and me she was also rather pleased. It just meant that there were fewer things to dust.

Rusty's Big Day

Long ago there lived a poor farmer called Fred, who had a horse called Rusty. Once Rusty had been a good, strong horse. He had willingly pulled the plough and taken his master into town to sell his vegetables. Now he was too old to work on the farm, but the farmer couldn't bear to think of getting rid of him because he was so sweet-natured. "It would be like turning away one of my own family," Fred used to say. Rusty spent his days grazing in the corner of the field. He was quite content, but he felt sad that he was no longer able to help the poor farmer earn his living.

One day, Fred decided to go to town to sell a few vegetables. He harnessed Beauty, the young mare, to the wagon and off they went. Beauty shook her fine mane and tossed a glance at Rusty as if to say, "Look who's queen of the farmyard!"

While Fred was in the town, his eye was caught by a notice pinned to a tree. It said:

Horse Parade at 2 pm today
The winner will pull the king's carriage
to the Grand Banquet tonight

"There's not a moment to lose, my girl!" said Fred. "We must get you ready for the parade." So saying, he turned the wagon around. "Giddy-up, Beauty!" he called, and she trotted all the way back to the farm.

Fred set to work to make Beauty look more lovely than she had ever done before. He scrubbed her hoofs and brushed her coat until it shone. Then he plaited her mane and tied it with a bright red ribbon. Rusty watched from the field. "How fine she looks," he thought, wistfully. "She's sure to win." He felt a bit sad that he was too old to take part in the parade, so he found a patch of the sweetest grass to graze on, to console himself.

All at once, he heard Fred approach. "Come on, old boy," he said, "you can come, too. It'll be fun for you to watch the parade, won't it?" Rusty was thrilled. It seemed such a long time since the master had last taken him into town. Fred brushed Rusty's coat, too. "You want to look your best, don't you now, old boy?" he said.

Soon the three of them set off back into town, with Fred riding on Beauty's back and Rusty walking by their side. When they reached the parade ground, there were already a lot of horses gathered there with their owners. There were horses of every shape and size – small, skinny ones, big, muscular ones and there were even big, skinny ones, too!

Soon it was time for the parade to begin. The king entered the parade ground, followed by the members of the royal court. They took their places at one end of the ground. Then the king announced three contests. First there would be a race. The horses would gallop from one end of the parade ground to the other. Then there would be a contest of strength. Each horse would have to try and pull a heavy carriage. Lastly, there would be a trotting competition. Each horse would have to carry a rider around the parade ground.

The competition began. All the horses lined up at the starting line. "Come on, Rusty. Have a go!" whispered Fred. He led Rusty and Beauty to where the other horses were lined up.

All the other horses turned and stared. "What's an old horse like you doing taking part in a contest like this?" one of them asked disdainfully.

"You won't make it past the starting line!" taunted another.

Rusty said nothing and took his place at the start. Then they were off down the field. Rusty felt his heart pounding and his feet fly like never before, but try as he might he just couldn't keep up with the others and came in last.

"What did you expect?" snorted the other horses turning their backs on poor old Rusty.

However, Rusty was not downcast. "Speed isn't everything," he said to himself.

Now it was time for the test of strength. One by one the horses took it in turns to pull the carriage. When it was Rusty's turn, he tried his best. He felt every muscle in his aching body strain, as he slowly pulled the carriage along.

"Not a hope!" declared the other horses.

"Strength isn't everything," said Rusty to himself.

Next it was time for the trotting competition. "I shall ride each horse in turn," declared the king. He climbed up on to the first horse, but it bolted away so fast that the king was left hanging by the stirrups. The next horse lifted his legs so high that he threw the king right up in the air and he might have hurt himself badly, if he hadn't been caught by one of his courtiers. The next horse was so nervous about carrying the king that his teeth chattered, and the king had to put his fingers in his ears. Then it was Beauty's turn and she carried the king magnificently, until she stumbled at the end. At last it was Rusty's turn. The other horses sniggered, "Let's see that old horse make a fool of himself!"

Rusty carried the king quite slowly and steadily, making sure he picked his feet up carefully, so that his royal highness would not be jolted. "Thank you for a most pleasant ride," said the king dismounting. There was a hush as the horses and their owners awaited the result of the contest. "I have decided," announced the king, "that Rusty is the winner. Not only did he give me a most comfortable ride, but he accepted his other defeats with dignity. Speed and strength are not everything, you know."

Rusty and Fred were overjoyed, and even Beauty offered her congratulations. "Though I might have won if I hadn't stumbled," she muttered.

So Rusty proudly pulled the king's carriage that evening, and he made such a good job of it that the king asked him if he would do it again the following year. Then the king asked Fred if his daughter could ride Beauty from time to time. He even gave Fred a bag of gold to pay for the horses' upkeep. So the three of them were happy as they never had been before as they returned home to the farm that night.

Esmerelda the Ragdoll

At the back of the toy cupboard on a dark and dusty shelf lay
Esmerelda the ragdoll. She lay on her back and stared at the shelf
above, as she had done for a very long time. It seemed to
Esmerelda that it was many years since she had been lifted up by
Clara, her owner, and even longer since she had been out in the
playroom with the other toys. Now her lovely yellow hair was all
tangled and her beautiful blue dress was creased, torn and faded.
Each time Clara opened the toy cupboard door, Esmerelda hoped
very much that she would be chosen, but Clara always played
with the newer toys at the front of the cupboard. Every time
Clara put her toys back in the cupboard, Esmerelda felt herself
being pushed further towards the back. It was very uncomfortable
and indeed, Esmerelda might have suffocated if it wasn't for a
hole at the back of the cupboard, which enabled her to breathe.

These days Esmerelda felt very lonely. Until recently a one-eyed teddy bear had been beside her on the shelf. Then one day he had fallen through the hole at the back of the cupboard and was never seen again. Esmerelda missed him dreadfully, for he had been a lovely old teddy with a gentle nature. Now she, too, could feel herself being pushed towards the hole. She felt a mixture of excitement and fright at the prospect of falling through it. Sometimes she imagined that she would land on a soft feather bed belonging to a little girl who would really love her. At other times she thought that the hole led to a terrifying land full of monsters.

One day Esmerelda heard Clara's mother say, "Now Clara, today you must tidy up the toy cupboard and clear out all those old toys you no longer play with."

Esmerelda could see Clara's small hands reaching into the cupboard. She couldn't bear the thought of being picked up by the little girl and then discarded. "There's only one thing to do," she said to herself. She wriggled towards the hole, closed her eyes and jumped. Esmerelda felt herself falling, and then she landed with a bump on something soft.

"Watch out, my dear!" said a familiar voice from underneath her. Esmerelda opened her eyes and saw that she had landed on One-eyed Ted.

The two toys were so overjoyed to see each other again that they hugged one another. "What shall we do now?" cried Esmerelda.

"I have an idea," said Ted. "There's a rusty old toy car over there. I wanted to escape in it, but I can't drive with only one eye. What do you think? Shall we give it a go?"

"Yes, yes!" exclaimed Esmerelda, climbing into the driver's seat.

By now One-eyed Ted had found the key and was winding up the car. "Away we go!" he called as they sped off.

"Where are we going?" shouted Esmerelda.

"To the seaside," replied Ted.

"Which way is it?" asked Esmerelda, holding on to her yellow hair streaming behind her in the wind.

"I don't know. We'll have to ask the way," said Ted.

Rounding a bend, they came across a black cat crossing the road. "Excuse me," called Ted, "could you tell us the way to the seaside?"

Now, as you know, cats hate water. "Whatever do they want to go near water for? Why should I help them?" thought the cat. "It's the other side of that mountain," he growled as he ran off.

On sped the rusty car, and up the mountainside. When they reached the top of the mountain they met a sheep. Now, as you know, sheep never listen properly. "Excuse me," said Esmerelda, "where can we find the beach?"

Well, the silly sheep thought Esmerelda was asking where they could find a peach! "Down there," she bleated, nodding towards an orchard in the valley below.

Esmerelda and Ted leaped back into the car and sped off down the mountainside, but when they reached the orchard there was no sign of water, of course – just a lot of peach trees.

Once again they scratched their heads in puzzlement.
Just then a mole popped his head out of the earth.
"Excuse me," said Ted, "would you happen to
know how we can find the seaside?"

Now the mole was very wise, but
unfortunately he was also, as you
know, very short sighted. He peered at Esmerelda's blue dress.
"That patch of blue must surely be a river, and rivers run into
the sea," he thought.

"Just follow that river," he said, "and you'll end up at the seaside.
Good day!" And with that he disappeared under ground again.

Esmerelda and Ted looked even more puzzled, for there was
no sign of a river in the orchard. "Oh well," sighed Esmerelda,
"perhaps we'll never find the seaside."

"Don't give up," said Ted. "We'll surely find it in the end." They
climbed back in the rusty car and set off again. After a short while
the car started to splutter and then it came to a complete halt at
the side of the road. "What shall we do now?" cried Esmerelda.

"We'll just have to wait here and see what happens," said Ted.
It seemed like a very long time that they sat beside the road. At
long last they heard footsteps, and then Esmerelda felt herself
being picked up.

"Look – it's a dear old tatty ragdoll," said a voice. Esmerelda
looked up and saw that she was being carried by a little girl.

Ted and the rusty car had been picked up by the girl's father. "We'll take them home and look after them," the man said.

Now they were in a real car and before long the toys found themselves in a house. The little girl carried Esmerelda, One-eyed Ted and the rusty car upstairs to her bedroom and put them down on a window sill. "I'll be back soon," she whispered.

Esmerelda looked out of the window and nearly danced for joy. "Look, look Ted," she shouted. For out of the window she could see the road, and beyond the road was a beach and then the sea. "We reached the seaside after all," she cried.

Esmerelda, Ted and the rusty car lived happily in the house beside the sea. Esmerelda's hair was brushed and plaited and she was given a beautiful new dress. Ted had a new eye sewn on and could see properly again. The rusty car was painted and oiled. Most days the little girl took her new toys down to the beach to play with, and the days in the dark toy cupboard were soon forgotten. The little girl used to tell her friends the story of how she had found her three best toys lying beside the road one day. And as for the toys, well, they sometimes talked about that strange day when they had such an adventure – and they'd burst out laughing.

The Wolf and the Seven Goats

There was once an old mother goat who had seven little goats. They all lived in a tiny house on the edge of a big, dark forest. One day, the mother goat had to go into the forest to collect food. Before she left, she called her seven little goats to her and said, "Now, children, promise me that while I am away you will lock the door and be on your guard against the wicked wolf. If you see him, don't let him in, because he would certainly eat you all up. You can recognize him by his gruff voice and his big black paws."

"Yes, mother," the little goats replied, "we promise to be very careful."

So the mother goat trotted cheerfully away into the forest, and the little goats locked the door. Some time later, there was a knock at the door, and the little goats heard a voice calling, "Open the door, children, it is your mother. I have brought back a present for each of you."

But the little goats heard that the voice was gruff, and not the gentle voice of their mother, and so they called, "No, we will not let you in! You do not have a soft voice like our mother's, you have a gruff voice. You are the wolf!"

So the cunning wolf went to a shop and stole a jar of syrup and swallowed it to make his voice soft. Then back he went to the little house by the forest. "Open the door, children," he called in his new, soft voice. "It is your mother. I have brought back a present for each of you."

Now the little goats heard the soft voice, but in his eagerness to get into the house the wolf had put his big black paws on to the window ledge, and so the little goats cried out, "No, we will not let you in! Our mother has beautiful white feet, but you have black feet. You are the wolf!"

So the wolf ran back into the village and went to the baker's shop, where he stole some flour and covered his paws in it. The wolf ran back to the little house by the forest. "Children, children, open the door!" he called again. "It is your mother. I have brought back a present for each of you."

32

The little goats heard the soft voice but they could not see any paws, and they called out, "Let us see your paws so that we know you really are our mother." So the wolf lifted up his paws, which of course were all white from the flour plastered on them. The little goats thought that this time it really was their mother, and they unlocked the door.

The wolf rushed in. The little goats screamed and tried to hide. One jumped into a drawer; the second squeezed under the bed; the third buried itself in the bedclothes; the fourth leaped into a cupboard; the fifth went into the oven; the sixth hid under a basin; and the littlest one slipped inside the grandfather clock. But the wolf found them and gobbled them up – all except the youngest one hiding in the grandfather clock. When the wolf had finished his meal, he felt very full and very sleepy. He wandered out of the house into a nearby meadow, lay down on some dry leaves, and promptly fell asleep.

When the mother goat came home from the forest, imagine her horror as she saw the door open, the furniture strewn around the house and the little goats all gone. She started calling them by name, but nobody answered until she called out the name of the youngest little goat, who was still hiding in the grandfather clock. She quickly pulled him out, and then he told her what had happened to all his brothers and sisters.

She ran out of the house with the little goat trotting beside her and soon found the wolf sleeping in the meadow. She looked carefully at him and saw that there were six lumps in his fat stomach, and that they seemed to be moving. "My little goats are still alive," she exclaimed with joy.

Quickly she sent the youngest goat back to her house for scissors, needle and thread. Then, while the wolf was still sleeping, she carefully cut a hole in the wolf's stomach. Soon a little goat popped out and then another and another, until all six were free and jumping for joy. They had not come to any harm, for in his greed the wolf had swallowed them all whole.

"Quick," cried the mother goat, "fetch me some rocks from the river so that I can fill up this wicked wolf's stomach." So the little goats each fetched a rock and the mother goat sewed them up inside the wolf's stomach.

When the wolf awoke, he was very thirsty. "What is the matter with me?" he thought. "I shouldn't have eaten all those goats at once. Now I've got indigestion." He set out to drink from the river. But his stomach was so heavy he could hardly walk and he staggered to the water's edge. As he bent over to drink, the weight of the stones pulled the wolf into the water, where he sank straight to the bottom and drowned. Then the mother goat and all her little goats – who had been watching – danced for joy. For never again would they be afraid of the wicked wolf!

The Giant Who Shrank

Once upon a time in a far-off land, there lived a huge giant.
He made his home in a big cave high up in the mountains.
His bed, table and chairs were made from great tree trunks.
And when he wanted a drink, he simply filled an old bath tub
with water and drank it down in one enormous gulp.
When he snored – which he did almost every night –
it sounded like a huge thunderstorm,
and the noise echoed all
around the mountains.

At the bottom of the mountains there was a village, but all the folk in the village were very different from the giant, for they were not big at all. They were just like you and me. They were afraid of the giant, of course, and whenever he came striding down the mountains to hunt, they all ran away into the woods or locked themselves inside their houses. Sometimes, the clumsy giant would tramp around the village squashing houses with his great feet as he went, and that only made the village folk even more frightened of him!

Although the giant was so big and strong, he was not a bad giant, but he was very, very lonely because everyone ran away whenever he appeared. Sometimes, while he was sitting alone in his cave, he could hear the villagers having feasts and parties and he longed to join them and be just like them.

One day, when the giant was tramping around the village as usual, something glinting in the sun caught his eye. At the top of a big tree (which of course was not very big as far as the giant was concerned) lay a gold box.

40

The giant bent down and picked up the box. To his surprise he heard a small voice inside say, "Help! Help! Let me out!"

The giant opened the box and out jumped an elf. "Thank you, thank you, large sir," he said. "I am a magic elf, but one of my spells went wrong and I got locked inside this box. No-one in the village could hear me calling for help high up in this tree."

To show his thanks, the elf said he would grant the giant one wish.

"I wish I could be the same as all the other villagers," boomed the giant.

"What a difficult wish," said the elf. "You are so big! But I will do my best." The elf closed his eyes and chanted a magic spell. But nothing seemed to happen – the giant was still as big as ever.

The giant was very sad to discover that he had not shrunk, but he wished the elf well, thanked him for trying and went on his way. As the giant was walking back to his cave in the mountains, he noticed something strange. All the puddles of water that he had passed on the way down to the village had got bigger. They were as big as lakes now! The giant looked up to see if it had been raining, but the sky was clear and blue.

Then another strange thing happened. The big stone steps he had cut in the mountain side leading up to his cave had also got bigger! He could hardly clamber up them.

Eventually, puffing and panting, the giant reached the door to his cave. But he could not reach the door knob. It now towered above him, far from his reach.

"What is happening?" thought the giant. "The elf's spell must have gone wrong. Not only am I still a giant, but everything around me has now got even bigger."

Suddenly the truth came to him. Of course! Everything had not become bigger – he had become smaller! The spell had worked after all. Now he was just the same as the other folk in the village.

He made his way to the village, wondering if everyone would still run away as before. But he need not have worried. All the village folk welcomed him into the village, and he lived there happily among them for the rest of his days.

The Bear and the Ice Kingdom

Once upon a time a king ruled a far-off land. It was a sunny, pleasant kingdom with lush forests, green meadows and sparkling rivers. The king of this land had a daughter he loved very much, and who one day would rule the kingdom.

Beyond the king's land was another kingdom, but this one was very different. It was an icy-cold place with wind-swept, snowy plains and cold, frozen seas. The sun never warmed this kingdom, and it was always winter. Anyone or anything venturing into the kingdom was immediately turned to ice by the cold. This kingdom was ruled by a wicked ogre, whose wish was to own the warm lands of his neighbour.

One day the wicked ogre thought of a cunning plan to capture the kingdom he desired. He decided he would kidnap the king's daughter. Once she had entered the wicked ogre's ice kingdom she, too, would be turned to ice. In time, the king would die and, as there would be no-one to inherit his kingdom, the wicked ogre could seize it.

So one day, the wicked ogre left his own cold kingdom and travelled to the other kingdom disguised as a merchant. He carried a big bag containing some samples of cloth and some jewellery. The wicked ogre came to the castle gates and asked if he might show the princess his wares. She agreed, and showed him to a room where he laid out the cloth and jewellery on a table. But as soon as she started to look at the wares, the wicked ogre bundled her up in the bag and carried her off.

As soon as the princess felt the cold chill of the wicked ogre's kingdom, she was immediately frozen to ice.

The wicked ogre thought that all he now had to do was wait for the king to die of old age or a broken heart, and the kingdom would be his. But despite the cunning of the wicked ogre, his evil deed had been spotted by one of the king's courtiers. The king immediately sent his troops to the ice kingdom to rescue his daughter. But as soon as they reached the kingdom they, too, were frozen to ice.

The king was in despair. There seemed to be no way to get his beloved daughter back. Then one day he thought of an idea. He sent out a royal proclamation to every part of his land. It said that anyone who could rescue his daughter would be granted any gift within the king's power to bestow.

Many adventurers tried to rescue the king's daughter, in the hope that they might win her hand in marriage, or be granted riches and lands as a reward. But each who ventured into the evil ogre's ice kingdom met the same fate. All were turned to ice.

Then one day, the king's dancing bear read the royal proclamation and asked to speak with the king. "Your majesty," said the dancing bear, "I have a plan to rescue your daughter, the princess."

"And what is your plan?" asked the king.

"My plan is a secret, your majesty," said the dancing bear. "But if you will trust me, I promise she will be brought safely home."

The king agreed to let the dancing bear try and rescue his daughter. After all, every other attempt had ended in failure so what did he have to lose? The dancing bear was released from his chain and went off immediately to begin his task. He travelled day and night until finally he reached his destination – a cold, snowy place where his cousin lived. His cousin was not like the dancing bear, however. The dancing bear was small and brown, but his cousin was big and white. This bear loved the cold and snow, for he had a thick fur coat. He was a polar bear.

The dancing bear told his cousin what had befallen the king's daughter. The polar bear agreed to rescue her. The dancing bear couldn't wait to get going, for his cousin's snowy home was much too cold for him. Eventually they arrived back in the king's land, and the polar bear set off alone to try and rescue the princess.

Soon he reached the wicked ogre's ice kingdom. A freezing, icy wind blew all around the polar bear, but his thick, warm fur coat kept out the cold. Then a huge snow storm came up, but the polar bear just shook his fur and all the snow fell from him. On went the polar bear until he reached the wicked ogre's castle.

The ogre never expected that anyone would be able to enter his cold kingdom without being turned to ice, so he never even locked his doors. While the ogre was snoring in his bedroom, the polar bear searched stealthily around the castle until he found the frozen princess. He gently gathered her up, and they were just about to make their escape when the ogre awoke.

As the wicked ogre tried to snatch the princess away from the polar bear, the polar bear dealt the wicked ogre a mighty blow with his paw. The wicked ogre fell down dead. The polar bear then carried the princess away from the icy kingdom. As soon as she entered her father's warm kingdom again, she returned to life.

There was much rejoicing at the return of the king's daughter, of course, and the first thing the king did was to summon the dancing bear to him.

"You have kept you promise," the king said, "and now I will keep mine. What is your wish?"

"All I ask, your majesty, is that I am freed to roam the forests of your kingdom."

The king immediately granted his wish. And as a reward to the polar bear, he was given the ice kingdom as his own domain which, being so cold, suited him just fine!

49

The Boy Who Wished Too Much

There once was a young boy named Billy. He was a lucky lad, for he had parents who loved him, plenty of friends and a room full of toys. Behind his house was a rubbish tip. Billy had been forbidden to go there by his mother, but he used to stare at it out of the window. It looked such an exciting place to explore.

One day, Billy was staring at the rubbish tip, when he saw something gold-coloured gleaming in the sunlight. There, on the top of the tip, sat a brass lamp. Now Billy knew the tale of Aladdin, and he wondered if this lamp could possibly be magic, too. When his mother wasn't looking he slipped out of the back door, scrambled up the tip and snatched the lamp from the top.

Billy ran to the garden shed. It was quite dark inside, but Billy could see the brass of the lamp glowing softly in his hands. When his eyes had grown accustomed to the dark, he saw that the lamp was quite dirty. As he started to rub at the brass, there was a puff of smoke and the shed was filled with light. Billy closed his eyes tightly and when he opened them again, he found to his astonishment that there was a man standing there, dressed in a costume richly embroidered with gold and jewels. "I am the genie of the lamp," he said. "Are you by any chance Aladdin?"

"N… n… no, I'm Billy," stammered Billy, staring in disbelief.

"How very confusing," said the genie frowning. "I was told that the boy with the lamp was named Aladdin. Oh well, never mind! Now I'm here, I may as well grant you your wishes. You can have three, by the way."

At first Billy was so astonished he couldn't speak. Then he began to think hard. What would be the very best thing to wish for? He had an idea. "My first wish," he said, "is that I can have as many wishes as I want."

The genie looked rather taken aback, but then he smiled and said, "A wish is a wish. So be it!"

Billy could hardly believe his ears. Was he really going to get all his wishes granted? He decided to start with a really big wish, just in case the genie changed his mind later. "I wish I could have a purse that never runs out of money," he said.

Hey presto! There in his hand was a purse with five coins in it. Without remembering to thank the genie, Billy ran out of the shed and down the road to the sweet shop. He bought a large bag of sweets and took one of the coins out of his purse to pay for it. Then he peeped cautiously inside the purse, and sure enough there were still five coins.

The magic had worked! Billy ran back to the garden shed to get his next wish, but the genie had vanished. "That's not fair!" cried Billy, stamping his foot. Then he remembered the lamp. He seized it and rubbed at it furiously. Sure enough, the genie reappeared.

"Don't forget to share those sweets with your friends," he said.

"What is your wish, Billy?"

This time Billy, who was very fond of sweet things, said, "I wish I had a house made of chocolate!"

No sooner had he uttered the words than he found that he was standing outside a house made entirely of rich, creamy chocolate. Billy broke off the door knocker and nibbled at it. Yes, it really was made of the most delicious chocolate that he had ever tasted! Billy gorged himself until he began to feel quite sick. He lay down on the grass and closed his eyes. When he opened them again, the chocolate house had vanished and he was outside the garden shed once more. "It's not fair to take my chocolate house away. I want it back!" he complained, stamping his foot once again.

Billy went back into the shed. "This time I'll ask for something that lasts longer," he thought. He rubbed the lamp and there stood the genie again.

"You've got chocolate all around your mouth," said the genie disapprovingly. "What is your wish?"

53

"I wish I had a magic carpet to take me to faraway lands," said Billy. No sooner were the words out of his mouth than he could feel himself being lifted up and out of the shed on a lovely soft carpet. The carpet took Billy up, up and away over hills, mountains and seas to the end of the Earth. He saw camels in the desert, polar bears at the North Pole and whales far out at sea. At last, Billy began to feel homesick and he asked the magic carpet to take him home. Soon he was back in his own garden again.

Billy was beginning to feel very powerful and important. He began to wish for more and more things. He wished that he did not have to go to school – and so he didn't! He wished that he had a servant to clear up after him and a cook to make him special meals of sweet things – and a cook and a servant appeared.

Billy began to get very fat and lazy. His parents despaired at how spoiled he had become. His friends no longer came to play because he had grown so boastful.

One morning, Billy woke up, looked in the mirror and burst into tears. "I'm so lonely and unhappy!" he wailed. He realised that there was only one thing to do. He ran down to the garden shed, picked up the lamp and rubbed it.

"You don't look very happy," said the genie, giving him a concerned glance. "What is your wish?"

"I wish everything was back to normal," Billy blurted out, "and I wish I could have no more wishes!"

"A wise choice!" said the genie. "So be it. Goodbye, Billy!" And with that the genie vanished. Billy stepped out of the shed, and from then on everything was normal again. His parents cared for him, he went to school and his friends came to play once more. But Billy had learned his lesson. He never boasted again and he always shared his sweets and toys.

Snow White

In the middle of winter, a young queen sat sewing by an open window. As she looked up and saw the snow falling, she pricked her finger and three drops of blood fell on to the snow. The red of the blood on the white snow, framed by the black ebony window frame, was so striking that the queen made a wish that she could have a child that was as red as blood, as white as snow and as black as ebony.

In time the queen's wish came true. She gave birth to a baby girl with snow-white skin, blood-red lips and hair as black as ebony. The young queen died soon after the child was born, and the king named his daughter Snow White. Soon the king took a second wife, as beautiful as the first. But this one was also vain. She had a magic mirror and sometimes she stood in front of it and said, "Mirror, mirror, on the wall, who is the fairest of them all?"

And the mirror answered, "You are the fairest one of all."

Then the queen was happy because she knew that the mirror always told the truth.

Years passed and Snow White grew more and more beautiful. One day the queen stood in front of the mirror and asked, "Mirror, mirror, on the wall, who is the fairest of them all?"

And the mirror answered, "You were the fairest one, 'tis true, but now Snow White is lovelier than you."

From that moment on, the queen began to hate Snow White. She couldn't rest until she was rid of the girl, so she called her huntsman and said, "Take Snow White into the forest and kill her. And bring back her heart."

The huntsman could not bear to kill the little girl. He told Snow White to run away into the woods. "She won't survive for long without food and shelter," thought the huntsman with remorse. To satisfy the queen, he shot a wild boar and took back its heart.

Snow White went deeper into the woods until she was completely lost. At last she came to a house. Inside was a table with a white cloth laid for seven people, with food and drink at every place. Along one wall were seven beds covered with white quilts. Snow White was so hungry that she took a mouthful from each plate and a sip from each cup. Then she tried out all the beds but they were all too long, or too short, or too wide or too narrow – until she came to the last one of all, which was just right. She lay down and fell fast asleep. Some time later the owners of the house returned. They were seven dwarfs who worked all day mining gold in the mountains. They could soon tell that they had received a visitor.

"Someone's been sitting in my chair," said the first dwarf.

"And eating my food," said the second.

"And drinking my wine," said the third.

"And using my knife," said the fourth.

"And my fork," said the fifth.

"And my spoon," said the sixth.

"And she's asleep on my bed!" said the seventh dwarf.

The dwarfs all crowded around Snow White. She looked so comfortable that they let her sleep in peace.

In the morning, when Snow White woke up, she was frightened at first, but the dwarfs reassured her. She told them what had happened. "You can stay with us," they said. "You can clean our house, cook and wash for us and we will protect you." So Snow White stayed with the dwarfs. Each day when they went off to work they reminded her, "Don't let anyone in." And Snow White promised that she wouldn't.

For a while the queen felt happy again now that she thought Snow White was dead. Then one day, she stood in front of the mirror again and asked, "Mirror, mirror, on the wall, who is the fairest of them all?"

And the mirror answered, "Over the hills where the seven dwarfs dwell, Snow White is still alive and well. And though you are fairer than most, 'tis true, she is still far lovelier than you."

The queen was furious. "This time I'll finish her off myself," she screeched. Disguising herself as a pedlar she made the journey to the dwarfs' house. "Silks for sale. Ribbons and laces," she called.

Snow White looked out of the window and saw the fine things. "Surely it wouldn't hurt to look," she thought. She unlocked the door and chose a pretty lace.

"Let me thread it for you," offered the old woman. Then she laced Snow White's bodice so tightly that the girl couldn't breathe and she fell to the floor unconscious.

When the dwarfs returned that night, they found her and cut the laces. Snow White began to breathe again and soon she was able to tell them what had happened. "That was the queen," they told her, "and she'll be back."

For a while all was well, then again the queen stood in front of her mirror and asked, "Mirror, mirror, on the wall, who is the fairest of them all?"

And again the mirror answered, "Over the hills where the seven dwarfs dwell, Snow White is still alive and well. And though you are fairer than most, 'tis true, she is still far lovelier than you."

The queen was furious. This time she prepared a poisoned comb and set off for the dwarfs' house in a different disguise. "Come and buy my lovely combs," she called. This time Snow White refused to open the door. "Let me pass you one through the window," said the queen.

"Well there's no harm in that," thought Snow White, undoing the latch.

The queen leaned through the window. "Let me comb your lovely hair with this fine comb," she said. As soon as the comb touched Snow White's head, the poison began to work and she fell senseless to the ground.

The dwarfs came home to find Snow White lying on the floor. Carefully they removed the comb and she returned to life. Meanwhile, the queen returned to the castle and immediately went up to the mirror and repeated her question. Imagine her anger when she got the same reply as before. Now she prepared a special apple. One side was green, while the other was red. The queen poisoned the red half, then she set off for the dwarfs' house once more. This time she pretended to be a farmer's wife. Once again Snow White refused to open the door. "Don't worry," said the queen. "Have an apple anyway." She held out the poisoned apple.

"No, no, I mustn't," said Snow White, though the apple did look very tasty.

"Tell you what," said the queen, "we'll have half each."

"Well, it can't be poisoned," thought Snow White.

The queen carefully cut the apple in half. "Here, I'll have the sour green half and you have the nice sweet red half," she said. Snow White took the apple, but the moment she bit into it she fell down dead.

The queen hurried back to the castle and this time when she spoke to the mirror it replied, to her pleasure, "You are the fairest one of all."

The dwarfs came home and found Snow White. They wept bitterly when they saw that she was dead. They placed her in a glass coffin and set it on a hillside and took turns to guard her. One day a prince came upon the coffin. He was so moved by Snow White that he asked the dwarfs if he could take her with him. He was heartbroken when the dwarfs refused. In the end, they took pity upon him and agreed. As the prince's servants lifted the coffin, one of them stumbled. The apple dislodged itself from her throat and Snow White came back to life.

The prince asked Snow White to marry him and when she agreed, everyone was invited to the wedding, and nothing more was ever heard of the wicked queen.

No Hunting!

Mr Rabbit opened his eyes and gave a big yawn. He thought it seemed like the perfect day for going outside and nibbling some of the farmer's lettuces. And after that he thought he would go and see how well the farmer's carrots were growing, and maybe have a little nibble of those as well. He popped his head out of his burrow and looked this way and that, in case he saw any danger. Then he pricked up his ears and turned this way and that, in case he heard any danger. Finally, he sniffed the air this way and that, in case he smelled any danger. It seemed safe, so he hopped out of his burrow.

No sooner had he gone a couple of steps when "ZING" – a bullet whizzed past his head. Mr Rabbit jumped back into his burrow as fast as he could go, shaking with fright.

"Goodness, it's the rabbit hunting season," he gasped. He gathered his family of young rabbits around him and spoke to them. "Now children, listen very carefully," he said. "The rabbit hunting season has begun, so you must all stay safely inside the burrow until it's over. I will go out at night and forage for food for us all."

His children looked at him in dismay. "But it's lovely and sunny outside," they cried all together. "We'll be very careful."

But Mr Rabbit was having none of it. He insisted that they all stay under ground until the rabbit season was over.

For a few days, the young rabbits amused themselves as best they could by playing chase and hide and seek. But they were becoming very bored. Finally, they decided that they were going to do something to stop the rabbit hunting themselves.

First Tom, the eldest of Mr Rabbit's children, decided he would try and stop the hunters. So when it was dark, he crept out of the burrow and made his way towards the hunters' hut.

Although it was night and he was sure the hunters would be asleep, he was still very scared. Soon he came to the hut. It was standing in a clearing in the woods. It was dark inside the hut and he hoped the hunters were asleep. "If I can dig some big holes," he thought, "maybe they will fall into them in the morning and won't be able to get out until the hunting season is over."

So he dug and he dug like he had never dug before. Soon there were holes everywhere, right outside the door to the hunters' hut. Feeling very pleased with himself, but also very tired, Tom made his way back to the burrow just before it was light.

When the hunters awoke, they went straight out without falling down a single hole! Poor Tom, he had dug lots of holes alright, but the hunters' hut had two doors, and the hunters had simply gone out of the other one!

Then Jenny, the second oldest of Mr Rabbit's children, decided that she would try and stop the hunters. So when it was dark, she crept out of the burrow and made her way towards the hunters' hut. When she got there, she noticed that the window was open and so she decided to go inside. She, too, was very scared, but she thought about having to spend all those days in the burrow until the hunting season was over and that gave her the courage to carry on.

Inside the hut, she could see the hunters sleeping in their beds. She looked around, wondering what she could do to stop them hunting. Then suddenly she saw the hunters' clothes lying on a chair. Quick as a flash, she hopped up to them and started nibbling at them. In no time at all, the clothes were in shreds. "That'll stop them," thought Jenny. "They can't hunt without their clothes on!" Satisfied with her night's work, Jenny made her way back to the burrow just as dawn was breaking.

When the hunters awoke, they got straight up and went out hunting! Poor Jenny, she had chewed some clothes alright, but she had only chewed some spare clothes! The hunters had gone to bed wearing their other clothes in order to be out quickly in the morning.

Finally, Penelope, the youngest of Mr Rabbit's children, said she would try and stop the hunters.

"Don't be silly," said Tom to his sister. "You are far too young to be going out at night."

"And anyway," said Jenny, "what could you possibly think of doing to stop the hunters?"

"I'll think of something," said Penelope, who was really quite a clever little rabbit.

So that night, she crept out of the burrow and made her way to the hunters' hut. The window was open, just as before, and so Penelope hopped inside. She looked on the floor, she looked in the cupboards, and she looked under the beds, but she couldn't think of anything to stop the hunters.

Then she looked up and suddenly had an idea. For there on the table was a calendar, showing that very day's date. Penelope hopped on to the table and started to turn the pages. Finally she came to a page on the calendar that read: "RABBIT HUNTING SEASON ENDS TODAY". Satisfied with her work, Penelope hopped out of the hunters' hut and back home to her burrow.

In the morning, the hunters woke up, rubbed their eyes and got out of their beds. One of them glanced at the calendar. "Oh no!" he suddenly exclaimed. "Look at the date! The rabbit hunting season is over."

With that, the hunters (who were too silly to realise that someone else must have turned over the pages of the calendar) packed their belongings and went home. All was peace and quiet once more and the rabbits could hop about in the open air in safety.

The Toys That Ran Away

"Put your toys away, Lucy," said Lucy's mother from the kitchen, "it's time to get ready for bed."

Lucy gave a great big sigh. "Do I really have to?" she asked, knowing full well what the answer was going to be.

"Yes, of course you do," said her mother. "You shouldn't have to be told each time to put your toys away. You really don't look after them properly."

It was true. Lucy never had been very good at looking after her toys. Once she left her beautiful new doll outside in her pram and she had become ruined after it rained. Then she had carelessly dropped her tea set on the floor and some of the cups had broken. And she was forever just pushing all her toys back in the cupboard in a hurry, instead of putting them away carefully. Worse still, when she was in a temper, she would throw her toys, and sometimes she would even kick them.

Tonight Lucy was in another of her 'can't be bothered' moods. She grabbed a handful of toys and threw them into the cupboard. In first went some dolls, which all landed on their heads and then fell in a heap. Next Lucy threw in the little tables and chairs from the doll's house. They landed with a bounce and came to a stop in the corner. Without even looking behind her, Lucy then picked up some puzzles and a skipping rope, and tossed them into the cupboard, too. They landed with a crash on the floor of the cupboard as well.

"That's that," said Lucy. She closed the cupboard door, squashing the toys even more, and went into the bathroom to have her bath.

Inside the toy cupboard Teddy, one of the toys, spoke. "I'm not going to stay here a moment longer," he said.

"Nor me," said Katie the ragdoll.

71

"If we aren't going to be loved, we aren't staying either," chimed the doll's house furniture.

"I want to be somewhere where I'm not thrown around," said one of the puzzles.

"So do we," said the roller blades.

One after another, all the toys agreed that they weren't going to stay. They decided they would all go back to Toyland and wait to be given to some children who would love them more.

The next morning, Lucy decided that she would play with her skipping rope. When she opened the toy cupboard, she couldn't believe her eyes. All the toys had vanished. The shelves were completely empty.

At first Lucy thought her mother had moved them, but her mother said she hadn't. "I expect you've put them somewhere yourself, Lucy, and can't remember where you've left them," said her mother, not very helpfully. All day, Lucy searched high and low for her missing toys, but they were nowhere to be found. She went to bed in tears that night, wondering if she would ever be able to play with her toys again. She was already missing them terribly.

That night, Lucy was suddenly woken by a noise in her bedroom. Was she seeing things or was that a little fairy at the bottom of her bed? "Who are you?" asked Lucy.

"I am the special messenger from Toyland," replied the fairy. "I have been sent to tell you that all your toys have run away back to Toyland, because you treated them badly."

"Oh, I do miss my toys so much," cried Lucy.

"Well, if you really do, then you had better come and tell them yourself," said the fairy.

With that, the fairy floated over to Lucy and took her hand. The fairy then beat her wings so fast that they became a blur. At the same time Lucy felt herself being lifted from her bed. Out of Lucy's bedroom window they both flew, across fields and forests, until it became too misty for Lucy to see anything at all.

Suddenly, they were floating down to the ground. The mist lifted, and Lucy found herself in the grounds of a huge fairy-tale castle with tall, pointed turrets and warm, yellow lights twinkling from the windows.

73

"This is Toyland Castle," exclaimed the fairy, as she led Lucy to a large red door.

The fairy knocked on the door. "Do enter, please," said a voice.

Lucy found herself in a large, cosy room with a huge log fire. Sitting in the corner was a kindly looking little man wearing a carpenter's apron and holding a broken wooden doll. "Hello," he said, "you've come to ask your toys to return, haven't you?"

"Well... er... yes," said Lucy, not really quite knowing what to say.

"It's up to them to decide, of course," said the little man. "They only come back here if they are mistreated. If they are broken, I repair them, and then they go to other children who love them more."

"But I *do* love my toys," wept Lucy.

"Then come and tell them yourself," smiled the little man.

He led Lucy into another room, and there, to her surprise, were all her toys. Not only that, but they were all shiny and new again. Nothing was broken or chipped or scratched.

Lucy ran up to her toys. "Please, toys, please come home again. I really do love you and miss you, and I promise I shall never mistreat you again," she cried. She picked up Teddy and gave him a big hug. Then she did the same thing to all the other toys.

"Well, it's up to the toys now," said the little man. "You must go back home again with the fairy messenger and hope that they will give you another chance."

With that, the fairy messenger took Lucy's hand, and soon they were floating over her own garden again and through her bedroom window. Lucy was so tired she didn't even remember falling asleep when she got into bed.

In the morning she awoke, still rather sleepy, and rushed to the toy cupboard. There, neatly lined up on the shelves, were all her toys. Lucy was overjoyed. From that day on, she always treated her toys well and took great care of them.

Lucy never was quite sure whether the whole thing was a dream or not, but it certainly did the trick whatever it was. There was one thing that really puzzled her though. If it had just been a dream, why were all the toys so shiny and new again?

Mrs Mouse's Holiday

Mrs Mouse was very excited. All year she had been *so* busy. First there had been nuts and berries to gather in readiness for winter. Then she had needed to give her little house a big spring clean to make it nice and fresh. Now, as the warm sun shone down on the trees and flowers of her woodland home, she had promised herself a well-deserved holiday. But getting ready for holidays seemed to make one busier than ever! There was so much to do!

First she took out her little case, opened it and placed it carefully on her neatly made bed. Then she rushed to her cupboard and selected some fine holiday dresses. Back to her case she scuttled and laid them in. Now she chose several pairs of shoes – a nice pair of sandals for walking along the front in, a pair of smart shoes for shopping in, an even smarter pair for going to dinner in, and another pair just in case!

"I'll need a couple of sun hats," she thought to herself, and so into the case they went as well. These were followed by a coat, some gloves and a scarf (just in case the breeze got up and it became cold). Then, in case it became very sunny, in went some sunglasses, some sun cream and a sunshade. But, oh dear, there were so many things in the case that it refused to shut. She tried sitting on it, and bouncing on it, but still it stubbornly would not close.

So out from the case came all the things that she had just put in, and Mrs Mouse scurried to the cupboard again and chose an even bigger case. This time they all fitted perfectly, and she shut the case with a big sigh of relief.

Now she was ready to go to the seaside for her holiday. She sat on the train, with her case on the rack above her head, munching her hazel nut sandwiches and looking eagerly out of the window hoping to see the sea. Finally, as the train chuffed around a bend, there it was! A great, deep blue sea shimmering in the sun, with white gulls soaring over the cliffs and headlands.

"I'm really looking forward to a nice, quiet rest," she said to herself.

Her guest house was very comfortable, and so close to the sea that she could smell the clean, salty air whenever she opened her window. "This is the life," she thought. "Nice and peaceful."

After she had put her clothes away, she put on her little swimming costume and her sun hat and packed her beach bag. Now she was ready for some peaceful sunbathing!

At the beach, she found herself a quiet spot, closed her eyes and was soon fast asleep. But not for long! A family of voles had arrived on the beach, and they weren't trying to have a quiet time at all. The youngsters in the family yelled at the top of their voices, splashed water everywhere, and sent their beach ball tumbling all over Mrs Mouse's neatly laid out beach towel.

Just as Mrs Mouse thought that it couldn't get any noisier, along came a crowd of ferrets. Now if you've ever sat on a beach next to a crowd of ferrets, you'll know what it's like. Their noisy shouting and singing made Mrs Mouse's head buzz.

Mrs Mouse couldn't stand it a moment longer. She was just wondering where she might find some peace and quiet when she spotted a rock just a little way out to sea.

"If I swim out to that rock," she thought, "I will surely have some peace and quiet there." So she gathered up her belongings and swam over to the rock. It was a bit lumpy, but at least it was quiet. Soon she was fast asleep again.

Just then the rock started to move slowly out to sea! It wasn't really a rock at all, you see, but a turtle which had been dozing near the surface. Off into the sunset it went, with Mrs Mouse dozing on its back, quite unaware of what was happening.

Eventually, the turtle came to a deserted island. At that moment, Mrs Mouse woke up. She looked at the empty beach, and without even knowing she had been sleeping on a turtle, she jumped off and swam to the shore, thinking it was the beach that she had just left.

Just then, the turtle swam off, and Mrs Mouse suddenly realised what had happened. For a moment she was horrified. But then she looked at the quiet, palm–fringed beach with no-one about but herself, and thought of the noisy beach she had just left.

"Well, perhaps this isn't such a bad place to spend a quiet holiday after all," she thought.

And that's just what she did. Day after day she lazed on her own private beach with no–one to disturb her. There were plenty of coconuts and fruits to eat, and she wanted for nothing. She even made herself a cozy bed from palm leaves.

Eventually, though, she started to miss her own little house in the woods and decided it was time to get back home. First she took half a coconut and nibbled out the tasty inside. "That will make a fine boat to sit in," she said.

Next she found a palm leaf and stuck it in the bottom of the shell. She took her little boat to the water's edge and, as the wind caught her palm leaf sail, off she floated back to the boarding house to get her belongings.

As she sailed back she thought, "This is the quietest holiday I've ever had. I may come back here next year!"

Rapunzel

There once lived a man and his wife who had long wished for a child. At last their wish was granted and the wife found that she was expecting a baby. At the back of their house was a garden that was filled with the most beautiful flowers and herbs. However, the man and his wife did not dare enter the garden, for it was owned by a wicked witch, of whom everyone was scared.

One day, when the woman was standing by her window looking down into the garden, she saw a flower bed full of the prettiest Rapunzel plants she had ever seen. They looked so fresh and green that she felt a great craving to eat some of them. Day after day she would sit by her window, staring at the Rapunzel plants for hours on end. Eventually she became quite pale and miserable.

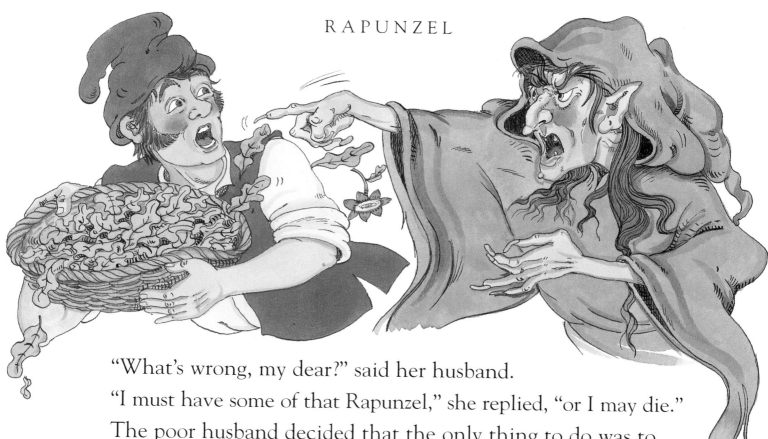

"What's wrong, my dear?" said her husband.

"I must have some of that Rapunzel," she replied, "or I may die."

The poor husband decided that the only thing to do was to steal into the witch's garden at night and take some of the plants. Late one night the man climbed the high wall that surrounded the garden and hastily snatched a bunch of Rapunzel plants and made off with them.

His wife was delighted. She made a salad of them that was so delicious that the next day she said to her husband, "I must have more of that delicious Rapunzel."

So that night the husband stole once more into the witch's garden. Imagine his horror when he dropped on to the grass to find the witch there lying in wait for him. "How dare you come into my garden and steal my Rapunzel plants," she shrieked. "You'll live to regret this."

"Please have mercy on me," begged the man. "I'm not really a thief. I came to help my wife, who is expecting our first child. She told me she would die if she didn't have some of your Rapunzel to eat."

Then the witch changed her tune. "By all means," she said, "take as much as you like. But in exchange you must give me the baby when it is born. Don't worry – I will care for it as if I were its mother. What do you say?" The man was so terrified that he hastily agreed to what the witch had said. When his wife gave birth to a baby girl the witch immediately appeared to take the child. The witch named her Rapunzel, after the plants that had caused all the trouble, and took the child away with her.

Rapunzel grew very beautiful, strong and healthy, with long golden hair that fell past her waist. When she was twelve years old the witch locked her away at the top of a tower in the middle of a forest. The tower had neither stairs nor a door, but only one window at the top so that nobody but the witch could reach her.

Each day when the witch visited her, she would stand below the girl's window and call out, "Rapunzel, Rapunzel, let down your hair, that I may climb without a stair."

Then the girl would wind her long tresses around the window hook and lower her hair all the way to the ground. The witch would climb up it as if it were a ladder. In this way, Rapunzel's lonely life went on for several years.

One day, a young prince was riding in the forest when he heard a sweet voice. It was Rapunzel singing to herself. The prince was so entranced that he followed the sound and came upon the tower.

But when he could find no way in he became discouraged and rode home. Rapunzel's lovely voice had stirred his heart so deeply, however, that he returned day after day to hear her singing.

One day, as he stood behind a tree, he saw the witch appear and heard her calling, "Rapunzel, Rapunzel, let down your hair, that I may climb without a stair."

Then he saw a mass of golden hair tumble down and watched the witch climb up it to the window. "Is that the way up?" thought the prince. "Then I will climb the golden ladder, too."

The next day, around dusk, the prince went to the tower and called, "Rapunzel, Rapunzel, let down your hair, that I may climb without a stair."

Immediately the tresses fell down and the prince climbed up. At first sight of the prince, Rapunzel was afraid, but the prince addressed her in such a friendly way that she knew she could trust him. "Once I had heard your voice," said the prince, "I couldn't rest until I saw you. Now I cannot rest until you agree to marry me."

Rapunzel by now had fallen truly in love with the young man, so she willingly accepted. "I wish I could come away with you," said Rapunzel. "You must bring some silk with you each time you visit, and I shall weave a ladder of silk and then I will be able to escape."

Each day the witch visited Rapunzel and each night the prince came. The witch suspected nothing until one day Rapunzel forgot herself and said to the witch, "Why are you so much heavier to pull up than the prince?"

"Oh, treacherous girl," screamed the witch. "You have deceived me!" She snatched up a pair of scissors and cut off all Rapunzel's lovely hair. Then the witch drove Rapunzel from the tower and left her in a wild and desolate place to fend for herself as best she could.

That night, along came the prince to the tower and said, as usual, "Rapunzel, Rapunzel, let down your hair, that I may climb without a stair."

But the witch was lying in wait. She tied Rapunzel's hair to the window hook and let the golden tresses fall to the ground. Up climbed the prince full of joy, as always. But when he stepped in through the window, it was not his beautiful Rapunzel that met his gaze but the icy glare of the witch. "Aha!" cried the witch with a sneer. "So you thought you could steal my girl, did you? Well she's gone and you'll never set eyes on her again."

Beside himself with grief, the prince threw himself from the tower and would have died had he not landed in the thickest briars. Although he survived, the thorns pierced his eyes and blinded him. For many years he wandered through the wilderness grieving for his lost Rapunzel and living on whatever he could find to eat. Eventually, he wandered into the same part of the wilderness where Rapunzel lived in miserable poverty with the twins she had borne.

Just as he had done so many years ago, the prince heard a sweet voice coming through the trees. He made his way towards the sound of the voice. Suddenly Rapunzel saw him and straight away she recognised him. She ran to him and threw her arms around him weeping. As she wept tears of joy and sorrow, two teardrops fell into his eyes, healing them and restoring his sight.

Then the two were united again and the prince took Rapunzel and their children back to his own kingdom, and they all lived happily ever after.

Jimbo Comes Home

Jimbo the circus elephant was snoring away in his cage one night when he heard a strange noise. At first he thought it was part of his dream. In his dream he was walking across a hot, dusty plain while in the distance there was the sound of thunder.

All at once Jimbo was wide awake. He realised that he was in his cage after all and that what he thought was the sound of thunder was the noise of his cage on the move. Now this worried him, because the circus never moved at night. He rose to his feet and looked around. He could see men pulling on the tow bar at the front of the cage. These were strangers – it certainly wasn't Carlos his trainer! Jimbo started to bellow, "Help! Stop thief!" But it was too late. His cage was already rumbling out of the circus ground and down the road.

Eventually, the cage passed through a gate marked 'Zipper's Circus' and Jimbo knew what had happened. He had been stolen by the Zipper family, his own circus family's greatest rivals! Jimbo was furious. How had the thieves got away with it? Surely someone at Ronaldo's Circus must have heard them stealing him? But Jimbo waited in vain to be rescued.

The next morning, the thieves opened up Jimbo's cage and tried to coax him out, but he stayed put. In the end, after much struggling, they managed to pull him out. Once he was out of his cage, he took the biggest drink of water he could from a bucket and soaked his new keeper! He refused to cooperate, kicked over his food, and when he appeared in the circus that night he made sure he got all the tricks wrong.

"Don't worry," said Mr Zipper to Jimbo's new trainer, "he'll just take a little while to settle down. Soon he'll forget that he was once part of Ronaldo's Circus." But Jimbo didn't forget for, as you know, an elephant never forgets.

The other animals in Zipper's Circus had all been stolen from other circuses, too. "You'll just have to get used to it here," said one of the chimps to Jimbo. "It's not so bad really." But Jimbo decided he was going to try and escape.

One night, a mouse passed by his cage. "Hello," called Jimbo mournfully, for by now he was feeling very lonely, and no-one had cleaned his cage out for days.

"Hello!" said the mouse. "You don't look very happy. What's the matter?" Jimbo explained how he had been stolen and wanted to escape back to his own circus. The mouse listened and then said, "I'll try to help." So saying, he scampered off and soon he was back with a bunch of keys. Jimbo was astonished. "Easy!" said the mouse. "The keeper was asleep, so I helped myself."

Jimbo took the keys in his trunk and unlocked the door to the cage. He was free! "Thank you!" he called to the mouse, who was already scurrying away.

Jimbo's first thought was to get back to his own circus as fast as possible. However, he wanted to teach those thieves a lesson. He could hear them snoring in their caravan. He tiptoed up, as quietly as an elephant can tiptoe, and slid into the horse's harness at the front. "Hey, what do you think you're doing?"

neighed one of the horses, but Jimbo was already hauling the robbers' caravan out of the gate and down the road.

So gently did he pull the caravan that the thieves never once woke up. Eventually they reached Ronaldo's Circus. Mr Ronaldo was dumbstruck to see Jimbo pulling a caravan just like a horse! Mr Ronaldo walked over to the caravan and was astonished to see the robbers still fast asleep. He raced to the telephone and called the police, and it wasn't until they heard the police siren that the robbers woke up. By then it was too late. As they emerged from the caravan scratching and shaking their heads they were arrested on the spot and taken off to jail. "There are a few questions we would like to ask Mr Zipper regarding the theft of some other circus animals, too," said one of the police officers.

Mr Ronaldo, and Jimbo's keeper Carlos, were both delighted to see Jimbo back home again. And Jimbo was just as delighted to be back home. Then Mr Ronaldo and Carlos started whispering to each other and began walking away looking secretive. "We'll be back soon, we promise," they said to Jimbo. When they returned, they were pushing Jimbo's old cage. It had been freshly painted, there was clean, sweet-smelling straw inside, but best of all there was no lock on the door! "Now you can come and go as you please," said Carlos.

And Jimbo trumpeted long and loud with his trunk held high, which Carlos knew was his way of saying, "THANK YOU!"

The Mean King and the Crafty Lad

There was once a king who was as mean as he was rich. He lived in a great palace where he spent his days counting his bags of gold coins. Meanwhile his subjects lived in great poverty. Sometimes the king would summon his page to prepare the royal carriage. Then the king would set forth in his great, golden coach to survey his kingdom.

Now not only was the king extremely rich, but he was very vain. As he passed his subjects working in the field, he liked them to bow to him and pay him compliments. "How handsome you look today, your majesty!" they would call, or "How well the colour pink suits you, Sire!"

His head would swell with pride as he moved on. "My people truly adore me!" he would say.

But for all their complimentary words, the people
hated their king. They resented the fact that the king
lived in splendour while his subjects toiled hard all their
lives. At last a secret meeting was called among the
peasants. "Let's sign a petition demanding our rights!"
cried one man.

"And fair pay!" shouted another. They all cheered and
clapped their hands.

"Who's going to write down our demands?" called an old
woman. Now the crowd was hushed, for none of them knew how
to read or write.

"I know what we can do instead," called a voice from the
back. Everyone turned round to see a young lad in rags. "Let's
march on the palace!" he cried.

"Yes!" roared the crowd.

As the angry mob reached the palace, the king saw them and
sent out his guard dogs. The peasants were forced to flee for their
lives with the dogs snapping at their ankles. Not until the last
peasant was out of sight did the king call off his dogs.

"Good work!" he cried.

From then on, however, life became even harder for the people because the king was on his guard in case they marched on the castle again. Now, when he went out and about in his kingdom, he was always accompanied by his hounds.

Eventually, another secret meeting was called. "What can we do?" the people said. "We will never be able to get past those savage dogs."

"I've got an idea," came a familiar voice. It was the ragged lad again. For a while there was uproar as folk accused him of having nearly lost them their lives. "Please trust me," pleaded the lad. "I know I let you down, but this time I've got a well thought-out plan to get the king to give up his money." In the end, the peasants listened to the boy's scheme and decided to let him try.

The next day, the boy hid in a branch of a tree that overhung the palace garden. With him he had some dog biscuits, in which he had hidden a powerful sleeping pill. He threw the biscuits on to the palace lawn and waited. Some time later, as the boy had hoped, the king's hounds came out on to the lawn. They headed straight for the biscuits and gobbled them up. Soon they were fast asleep, one and all.

Quickly the lad slid out of the tree and, donning a large black cape, he ran round to the front of the palace and rapped on the door. A sentry opened the door. "Good day," said the lad, "I am Victor, the world-famous vet. Do you have any animals requiring medical attention?"

"No," replied the sentry, slamming the door in the lad's face. Just then voices could be heard from within the palace. After a few moments, the sentry opened the door again and said, "As a matter of fact, we do have a bit of a problem. Step inside."

The sentry led the lad out to the lawn where the king was weeping over the dogs' bodies. "Oh, please help," he cried. "I need my dogs. Without them I may be besieged by my own people."

The lad pretended to examine the dogs. He said to the king, "I have only seen one case like this before. The only cure is to feed the animals liquid gold."

"Liquid gold?" exclaimed the king. "Wherever shall I find liquid gold?"

"Fear not," said the lad, "I have a friend – a witch – who lives in the mountains. She can turn gold coins into liquid gold. You must let me take the dogs – and a bag of gold – to her and she will cure them."

Well, the king was so beside himself with fear that he readily agreed. The sleeping dogs were loaded on to a horse-drawn cart, and the king gave the lad a bag of gold saying, "Hurry back, my dogs are most precious."

Off went the lad, back to his home. His mother and father helped him unload the dogs, who by now were beginning to wake up. They took great care of the dogs, who were glad to be looked after kindly for once. The next day the lad put on the cloak again and returned to the palace. "The good news is," he said to the king, "that the cure is working. The bad news is that there was only enough gold to revive one dog. I'll need all the gold you've got to cure the others."

"Take it all," screamed the king, "only I must have my dogs back tomorrow!" He opened the safe and threw his entire stock of gold on to another cart, which the young lad dragged away.

That night the lad gave each of the king's subjects a bag of gold. The next morning he led the dogs back to the palace. To his surprise, the king didn't want them back. "Now I have no gold," he said, "I don't need guard dogs."

Then the lad saw that the king had learned his lesson, and he told the king what had really happened. And to everyone's joy, the king said the peasants could keep their bags of gold. As for the king, he kept the dogs as pets and became a much nicer person.

The Dog With No Voice

There once lived a prince whose words were pure poetry. He amused the court with his witty, rhyming verse, yet his kind and thoughtful words made him popular with all. It was said he could even charm the birds from the trees.

One day, he was walking in the forest when he came upon an old lady with a huge bundle on her back. "Let me help," said the prince. He took the load and walked along beside the woman. They chatted away and before long they had reached the old lady's door.

Now the old lady – who was really a witch – had been listening intently to the prince's words. "What a fine voice he has!" she thought to herself. "I would like my own son to speak like that. Then maybe he could find himself a wealthy wife and we'd be rich for ever more!"

"You must be thirsty," she said to the prince. "Let me give you something to quench your thirst to repay you for your kindness." The prince gratefully accepted, and was given a delicious drink which he drained to the last drop. He was about to thank the witch when he began to feel very peculiar. He found he was getting smaller and smaller. He looked down at his feet and saw two hairy paws. Then he turned round and saw to his horror that he had grown a shaggy tail! He tried to shout at the witch but all that came out of his mouth was a loud bark!

The witch hugged herself for joy. "My spell worked!" she cackled. "Come here my son!" she called.

There appeared at the door a rough-looking young man. "What's going on, my dearest mother?" he said in a voice that sounded familiar to the prince. Then he looked down and exclaimed, "Where did you find this poor little dog?"

Now the prince understood what had happened. "The old lady has turned me into a humble hound and given my voice to her son. Whatever am I to do?" he thought miserably. "I can't return to the palace. They'll never let a stray dog in." He turned with his tail between his legs and trotted off forlornly into the forest.

The witch and her son were delighted with his new voice. She made him scrub himself clean from top to toe and dressed him in the prince's clothes. "Now go," she said, "and don't return until you've found a rich girl to marry!"

The young man set off, eager to try out his new voice. Soon he was feeling very pleased with himself as he talked to passers-by. "What a very polite young man!" and "What a wonderful way with words," folk cried. "He could charm the birds out of the trees," other people said.

The witch's son travelled far and wide until at last he came to a castle where he spied a fair princess sitting on her balcony. He called to her and straight away she arose and looked down into the garden, enraptured by the sound of his beautiful voice. She was enchanted by his fine words and guessed they must belong to a prince. Soon the princess and the witch's son were chatting away merrily, and to his delight when he asked her to marry him she readily agreed. "For one with so beautiful a voice," she thought to herself, "must indeed be a fine young man."

Meanwhile, the poor dog-prince wandered in the forest, surviving as best he could by foraging for roots and fruits in the undergrowth. Feeling truly miserable, he stopped to drink from a stream. As he dipped his long dog's tongue in the cool water, he caught sight of someone sitting on a bridge. It was a pixie, fishing with a tiny net.

"Cheer up!" said the little fellow, "I saw everything that happened and I think I know how we can get your voice back. Follow me!" And with that he was off, dancing away through the forest with the dog-prince trotting along behind. They seemed to go on forever, and the dog-prince was feeling very hot, and the pads of his paws were quite sore, by the time they reached the castle. He could see the witch's son in the garden calling to the princess on the balcony. The dog-prince's eyes filled with tears, for she was quite the loveliest girl he had ever seen and he wished he could marry her himself.

"We will be married today," the witch's son was saying in the prince's voice, "I will await you by the church, my fairest one." Seizing his fishing net, the pixie leaped high in the air. As the words 'my fairest one' floated up to the balcony, he caught them in the net and gave them back to the dog-prince.

As soon as he had swallowed the words, the dog-prince could speak again. "Thank you, little pixie," he cried, "but what can I do? Now I am a dog with a prince's voice. The princess will never marry me."

"If you want to break the witch's spell, you must go to the church – fast!" said the pixie. And with those words he disappeared.

Straight away, the dog-prince ran to the church door. There was the princess looking most perplexed, for standing beside her was the witch's son – with not a word in his head. "I don't understand," she cried, "I thought I was to marry a silver–tongued young man, but now I find he is a dumb ragamuffin!"

"I can explain," exclaimed the dog-prince.

The princess spun around. "Who can explain?" she asked, for all she could see was a dog in front of her. "What a handsome dog!" she cried, bending down and kissing him on the nose. To her astonishment, the dog's hairy paws and shaggy tail immediately disappeared and there stood the prince. "But you're... but he..." she stammered looking from the prince to the witch's son.

Well, the prince explained everything that had happened, and after that he and the princess were married with great rejoicing. And as for the witch's son? He wasn't a bad young man, really, so the prince taught him to speak again – with a beautiful voice – and he married the princess's younger sister.

Jack and the Beanstalk

Once there was an old woman who lived with her only son Jack in a tumble-down cottage in a meadow by a pine forest. The old woman and her son were very poor, and they were getting poorer as each winter passed. After one particularly cruel and cold winter, when the ground had frozen like ice, the old woman turned to her son and said, "Jack, there is only one thing left to sell. You must take the old brown cow to market tomorrow and sell her for her meat – she is all that is left between us and starvation, so mind you get a good price!"

So the next morning Jack took the old brown cow and started the long journey into town.

Halfway through his journey, Jack stopped to eat his crust of bread. Just then a farmer passed by, and stopped to chat. After Jack told the farmer where he was heading and why, the farmer looked at the old cow and scratched his chin thoughtfully. He put his hand into his pocket and said to Jack, "I'll swap you these dried beans for your old brown cow."

Jack looked at the beans in the farmer's hand and shook his head. "I'm sorry," he said, "but I must take the old brown cow to sell at the market so that my mother and I can buy bread."

The farmer promised Jack that if he would swap the cow for the beans, Jack would make his fortune. Jack finally agreed, and went home with the beans in his pocket.

When he got home he told his mother about his adventure, but his mother cried when Jack told her the old brown cow was gone and all they had were dried beans. She snatched the beans from Jack's hand and threw them out of the window in anger.

Just as dawn was breaking, Jack woke up to discover a huge beanstalk had shot up during the night right outside his window. He ran downstairs and looked at the huge beanstalk – it was taller than even the tallest trees in the nearby pine forest, and disappeared into the clouds. Jack decided to climb the beanstalk.

Jack climbed and climbed. He climbed so high that when he looked down, the tumble-down cottage was a tiny speck far below. The top of the beanstalk was still out of sight so he climbed some more. Eventually, Jack climbed through the clouds and was amazed when he got to the top of the stalk to discover another land very different from the one he'd left below.

Everything was HUGE. The trees were enormous, the grass came up to Jack's shoulder, and in the distance was the largest castle he had ever seen. Just as Jack was starting out towards the castle, he heard a thunderous rustling in the grass behind him, and he looked round to see a huge giantess towering above him.

"Mmmmm – not much meat on those bones," she said, "so I won't bother to eat you. However, you might come in handy around the house to do all the boring old chores." And with that she picked Jack up and popped him into the pocket of her apron, and carried him into the castle. On the way, she warned Jack not to let her husband, the giant, see him. "The last house boy I had was made into jam, and he's looking for another to pound into bread," she said quite calmly.

Soon Jack felt the castle shudder at the approach of the giant, and he hid behind the coal scuttle. "Fee Fi Fo Fum," roared the giant. "I smell the blood of an Englishman. Be him live or be him dead, I'll break his bones to make my bread."

"Don't be silly," said the giantess, "you've never once changed your socks, and it's your feet you can smell."

Satisfied with this answer, the giant sat down and started to count his money. Jack sneaked a peek from his hiding place and saw a mountain of gold coins piled high on the table. Then the giant scooped it all back into the purse, put his feet on the table, and fell sound asleep.

When the thunderous snores convinced Jack that it was safe, he sneaked up on to the table. The purse was within reach, and Jack dragged it to the edge of the table where it fell with a tremendous KLUNK on to the floor. The giant slept on. Quickly Jack climbed down and dragged the purse to the castle door, and down to the meadow, and then down, down, down the beanstalk.

When Jack finally got back with his treasure he showed it to his mother who hugged him with joy, and warned him never to climb the beanstalk again.

But Jack decided that he would go back to the castle to find some more treasures, and when morning came again he got dressed and went down to the beanstalk to start the long climb all over again. Before he left the house, he tied a red scarf around his head, and painted freckles on his face, so that when he reached the top of the beanstalk and once again met the giantess, she would not recognise him.

Once again, she picked Jack up and popped him into her apron pocket, and warned him about the terrible giant. Once more, Jack hid as the castle trembled at the giant's approach.

"Fee Fi Fo Fum," roared the giant, "I smell the blood of an Englishman. Be him live or be him dead, I'll break his bones to make my bread."

"Tsk tsk," said the giantess, "the only thing you can smell is your armpits which have never been washed."

Satisfied with this answer, the giant sat down and called for his hen to be brought to him. Jack peeked around and saw to his amazement that the hen had laid a beautiful golden egg! Before long, the giant rested his head once more, then fell fast asleep.

When Jack heard the snoring, he sneaked up on to the table and gently took the hen, then quickly climbed down and carried it to the castle door, and down to the meadow and then down, down, down the beanstalk. When Jack returned once more with his treasure, his mother was waiting for him, and when Jack showed her the hen, she hugged him and begged him never to climb the beanstalk again.

But once again, Jack thought about the treasures in the castle, and the following morning he went down to the beanstalk to start the long climb all over again.

113

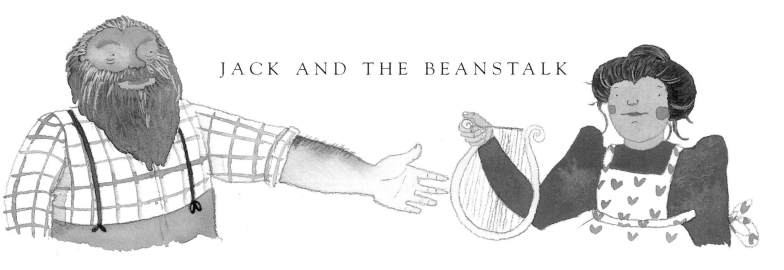

This time before he left the house, he tied a blue scarf around his head, and rubbed dirt into his face, and once again when he reached the top of the beanstalk and met the giantess, she did not recognise him. As before, she picked Jack up and popped him into her apron pocket, and warned him about the giant.

Again, the castle trembled at the approach of the giant. "Fee Fi Fo Fum. I smell the blood of an Englishman. Be him live or be him dead, I'll break his bones to make my bread," said the giant once again.

"What rot!" said the giantess. "That'll be all those bugs in your hair that's never been combed!"

Once more satisfied, the giant sat down and called for his harp to be brought to him. When the giant plucked at the strings of the harp, it magically started to sing in a clear soprano voice! The giant was soon lulled into a deep slumber across the table, and Jack wanted the beautiful harp so much that he didn't even wait for the snores! Jack climbed up to the table and put his hands on the harp to sneak it from under the nose of the sleeping giant, but to his horror, the harp started to shriek, "Help! Help! I'm being stolen."

The giant woke up. With a mighty roar he shouted, "Fee Fi Fo Fum, I smell the blood of an Englishman. Be him live or be him dead, I'll break his bones to make my bread." And with that he raced after Jack. But the giant wasn't as nimble as Jack, and Jack was able to rush out of the castle, down to the meadow and reach the top of the beanstalk with the giant in pursuit. Jack climbed down as quickly as possible, but the giant was not far behind him. The further down Jack climbed, the closer the giant got to him. When Jack was nearly at the bottom, he called to his mother to fetch the wood axe, and then Jack jumped the rest of the way to the ground. He grabbed at the axe and started to chop furiously at the stalk. The giant was almost down when the beanstalk crashed to the ground – right on top of him! The giant was squashed to nothing.

Now, with all the gold they had, Jack and his mother never needed to worry about money again.

Mr Squirrel Won't Sleep

It was autumn. The leaves were falling from the trees in the forest and there was a cold nip in the air. All the animals began to get ready for winter.

One night Mr Fox came back from hunting and said to his wife, "There's not much food about now it's getting colder. We'd better start storing what we can to help tide us over the winter."

"You're right, Mr Fox," replied his wife, as she gathered her cubs into their lair.

"I'd love to go fishing," said Mr Bear, "but I'll have to wait until spring now." He went into his den, shut the door tight and sealed it.

"Well, I'm off for a holiday in the sun," announced Mrs Cuckoo, preening her feathers. "See you all next year!" she called as she took to the wing and flew south.

Mrs Mouse ran by with a mouthful of straw. "Must dash," she squeaked, "or my winter bed will never be finished in time." But soon she, too, was curled up with her tail wrapped around her for warmth.

Now only Mr Squirrel wasn't ready for winter. He danced about in his tree, leaping from branch to branch and chasing his tail. "Ha, ha!" he boasted. "I don't have to get ready for winter. I have a fine store of nuts hidden away, a beautiful bushy tail to keep me warm and besides, I don't feel in the least bit sleepy." And he carried on playing in his tree.

"Are you still awake?" snapped Mr Fox.

"Go to sleep!" growled Mr Bear.

"Please be quiet," squeaked Mrs Mouse, drawing her tail more tightly about her ears.

But Mr Squirrel wouldn't go to sleep. Not a bit of it. He danced up and down all the more and shouted, "I'm having SUCH FUN!" at the top of his voice.

Winter came. The wind whistled in the trees' bare branches, the sky turned grey and it became bitterly cold. Then it started to snow. At first Mr Squirrel had a grand time making snowballs – but there was no-one around to throw them at and he began to feel rather lonely. Soon he felt cold and hungry, too.

"No problem!" he said to himself. "I'll have some nice nuts to eat. Now, where did I bury them?" He scampered down his tree to find that the ground was deep with snow. He ran this way and that trying to find his hiding places, but all the forest looked the same in the snow and soon he was hopelessly lost.

"Whatever shall I do?" he whimpered, for now he was shivering with cold and hunger and his beautiful, bushy tail was all wet and bedraggled.

All of a sudden he thought he heard a small voice. But where was it coming from? He looked all around but there was no sign of anyone. Then he realised that the voice was coming from under the snow. "Hurry up!" said the voice. "You can join me down here, but you'll have to dig a path to my door."

Mr Squirrel started digging frantically with his front paws and sure enough there was a path leading to a door under a tree stump. The door was slightly open – open enough for Mr Squirrel to squeeze his thin, tired body through.

Inside was a warm, cosy room with a roaring fire, and sitting by the fire was a tiny elf. "I heard you running around up there and thought you might be in need of a bit of shelter," said the elf. "Come and warm yourself by the fire." Mr Squirrel was only too pleased to accept and soon he was feeling warm and dry.

"This isn't my house, you know," said the elf. "I think it might be part of an old badgers' sett. I got lost in the forest and so when I found this place, I decided to stay here until spring. Though how I'll ever find my way home, I don't know." A fat tear rolled down the elf's cheek.

"I have been a very foolish squirrel," said Mr Squirrel. "If you hadn't taken me in I surely would have died. I am indebted to you and if you will let me stay here until spring, I will help you find your way home."

"Of course you can stay," replied the elf. "I'd be glad of the company." So Mr Squirrel settled down with his tail for a blanket and soon he was fast asleep.

Days and nights passed, until one day the elf popped his head out of the door and exclaimed, "The snow has melted, spring is coming. Wake up, Mr Squirrel." Mr Squirrel rubbed his eyes and looked out. It was true. There were patches of blue in the sky and he could hear a bird singing.

"Climb upon my back," Mr Squirrel said to the elf. "I'm going to show you the world." They set off through the forest until they came to the highest tree of all.

"Hold tight!" called Mr Squirrel as he climbed up through the branches until finally they reached the very top of the tree.

"You can look now," said Mr Squirrel, seeing that the elf had put his tiny hands over his eyes. The elf uncovered his eyes and stared and stared. He had never seen anything like it in his whole life. Stretching in all directions, as far as the eye could see, were mountains, lakes, rivers, forests and fields.

"What's that silvery-blue thing in the distance?" asked the elf.

"Why, that's the sea!" replied Mr Squirrel.

Suddenly the elf started to jump for joy.

"What is it?" said Mr Squirrel.

"I… I… can see my home," cried the elf, pointing down into the valley below the forest. "And there's my wife sitting in a chair in the sunshine. I must go home, Mr Squirrel. Thank you for showing me the world, for I should never have seen my home again without you." And with that he climbed down the tree and skipped all the way home.

Mr Squirrel made his way back to his own tree.

"Where have you been?" said Mr Fox.

"We've been looking for you," said Mr Bear.

"I'm glad you're home," said Mrs Mouse.

"So am I," said Mr Squirrel. "I've been very foolish, but I've learned my lesson. Now let's have a party – I've got rather a lot of nuts that need eating up!"

So the animals celebrated spring with a fine feast.

And Mr Squirrel vowed not to be silly again next winter.

The Sad Clown

Bongo the clown had a bit of a problem. Clowns were supposed to be happy, funny, jolly people, but Bongo was a very sad clown. Nothing at all seemed to make him laugh.

Whenever the circus came to town people from all around flocked to the big top hoping for an exciting day out. They thrilled to the daring performance of the high-wire act, as the acrobats leaped from one swinging trapeze to the next. They enjoyed the jugglers, who tossed bright, sparkling balls into the air while standing on one leg. And the crowd delighted in seeing the beautiful white horses parading around the circus ring with the bareback riders balancing on their backs. When the seals came on, there was always a big cheer from the crowd, for everyone loved them and could watch their clever antics for hours.

But the biggest favourite of the crowd, especially with all the children, was the clown. Dressed in his big baggy trousers he would enter the circus ring with his funny walk. Everyone laughed to see him. They laughed even more when they saw his big floppy hat with the revolving flower on it. Even his painted clown face made them laugh.

But when his act started, the crowd thought they would burst with laughter. First of all his bicycle fell apart as he tried to ride around the ring. Then he fell out of his motor car when the seat tipped up. By the time he had accidentally poured cold water down his trousers and fallen into the custard-filled swimming pool, the crowd were almost crying with laughter.

But beneath all the make-up, Bongo the sad clown wasn't smiling at all. In fact, he saw nothing funny at all in bicycles that fell apart as you used them, or cars that tipped you out as you went along, or having cold water poured down your trousers, or even ending up face first in a swimming pool full of custard. He simply hadn't got a sense of humour.

All the other performers in the circus decided they would try and cheer the sad clown up.

"I know," said the high-wire trapeze acrobat, "let's paint an even funnier face on him. That'll make him laugh."

So that's what they did, but Bongo still didn't laugh and was still just as sad.

"Let us perform some of our tricks, just for him," said the seals. So they sat on their stools and tossed their big coloured balls to each other, clapped their flippers together and made lots of honking sounds. But Bongo still didn't laugh. In fact, nothing that anyone tried made poor Bongo smile. He was still a very sad clown.

Then Percival the ring master spoke. "You know, I think I know what the problem is," he said. "There is nothing a clown likes better than playing tricks on other clowns. Perhaps if we had a second clown, that would cheer Bongo up."

So right away they hired another clown, called Piffle.

The circus arrived in the next town and soon it was time for Bongo and Piffle's act. Piffle started riding around on his bike while Bongo pretended to wash the car by throwing a bucket of water over it. Instead of the water landing on the car, of course, it went all over Piffle, who just happened to be cycling past at that moment. A little smile flickered across Bongo's face at the sight of the soaking wet Piffle.

Next, Bongo and Piffle pretended to be cooking, and Bongo tripped while carrying two huge custard pies. Both landed right in Piffle's face. Bongo let out a huge chuckle of laughter when he saw Piffle's custard-covered face.

THE SAD CLOWN

At the end of their act, the clowns were pretending to be decorators, painting up a ladder. Of course, you've guessed it. The ladders fell down and all the pots of paint landed on the two clowns. Bongo looked across at Piffle, who had a big paint pot stuck on his head, with paint dripping down his body. Bongo threw back his head and roared with laughter. Piffle thought Bongo looked just as funny with paint all over his body, too. And as for the crowd – well, they thought two clowns were even funnier than one and they clapped and cheered and filled the big top with laughter. After that Bongo was never a sad clown again.

Maurice the Minnow's Dangerous Journey

Maurice the minnow lived in a beautiful, reed-fringed pond in a clearing in the middle of a small woodland. He had been born one fine spring morning, and now he spent each day swimming happily in the shallows with all his little minnow brothers and sisters.

But life in the pond had its dangers, too! He had heard alarming stories about a kingfisher that would dive into the water from a branch overhanging the pond and grab tiny fish and swallow them down. And then there was the heron – a great, grey, stalking bird that suddenly loomed into the shallows and snatched unsuspecting fish with its great beak.

But the stories Maurice feared most were the ones about Lucius the pike. Lucius had lived in the pond for longer than anyone could remember. Woe betide you if you met Lucius when he was hungry, for he would dart out from his hiding place among the water weeds, and you would be gone! Nothing ever escaped from his huge jaws, which were lined with needle-sharp teeth. Maurice had heard tales of Lucius swallowing fish bigger than Maurice could imagine – not to mention ducks, voles and other animals of the pond. Why, there was even a rumour that Lucius had once snatched a dog from the bank and taken it down to the depths of the pond to devour it!

Maurice's mother had said that the best way to avoid meeting Lucius was to always stay in the shallows, and never swim across the pond, for it was in the deep, dark waters that Lucius loved to hunt.

One sunny summer's day, Maurice and his brothers and sisters were swimming in the shallows as usual, when suddenly he felt himself being lifted up and out of the water. The next thing he knew he was flapping helplessly in the bottom of a net, gasping for breath. Mercifully, he soon found himself back in the water again, but it seemed different now. It was light all around and there were no welcoming, sheltering weeds to hide in. And where were all his brothers and sisters? Next, to his horror, he saw a huge, unfamiliar creature staring at him. He'd heard no stories about anything as big as this! The creature's head seemed so close that Maurice felt certain he was about to be eaten. But just as suddenly the creature seemed to move away, and Maurice felt himself being carried along in this new, strange, watery world.

Maurice was wondering if he was to be trapped in this new, small pond forever when just as suddenly as he seemed to have entered the pond, he was now leaving it again. He felt himself falling down, down, until – with a splash – he was back in his own pond again. Or at least, it seemed like his pond, but nothing was quite as familiar as it had been. Finding a clump of water weed, he immediately dived under it for safety, while he considered what to do next.

"Hello, you're new here, aren't you?" a friendly voice said. Maurice looked round in surprise to find himself face to face with a frog. He told the frog about his horrible adventure while the frog listened patiently, nodding wisely from time to time.

"Well, we know what's happened to you, don't we?" said the frog when Maurice had finished. "You got caught in a little boy's fishing net. They're often about around here. I've no doubt the big creature you saw was just the little boy looking at you swimming in his jam jar full of water. And now he's decided to put you back. The only trouble is, you're far from home. You live on the other side of the pond. And to get you back means we have got to go on a very dangerous journey."

Maurice didn't like the sound of this at all, but he missed his family terribly and knew that he would never be able to get back home without the kind frog's help. So without more ado, the two of them set off for their journey across the deep, dark pond.

"Swim near the surface. It's safer," advised the frog, "but keep a close eye out for kingfishers."

They seemed to have been swimming for ages, when suddenly a great, dark shadow appeared beneath them.

"It's Lucius!" cried the frog in fright.

Before either of them could escape, they found themselves face to face with the dreaded pike. "Well, well," leered Lucius. "I can't believe my luck! A frog *and* a minnow. Lunch and supper together if I'm not mistaken!"

So saying, he opened his enormous jaws and was about to swallow them whole when – BOINK! – a huge, flat stone landed right on Lucius's head. Dazed, Lucius sank slowly towards the bottom of the pond.

"Quick! It's our chance to escape!" yelled the frog. The two friends swam for their lives. Maurice kept thinking that any moment Lucius would reappear, but he needn't have worried. Lucius had too big a headache to think about hunting for a while yet!

Then suddenly Maurice was home. He recognised his own little part of the pond, and there swimming in the shallows was his family.

"I can't thank you enough," said Maurice gratefully to the frog. "But what *did* happen to Lucius?"

"You can thank the little boy who caught you in the net for our escape," said the frog. "He was skimming stones across the pond and luckily Lucius's head got in the way!"

Maurice decided that he'd had quite enough adventures for one day, and found himself a cosy piece of water weed to hide under. Soon he was fast asleep.

Little Red Riding Hood

There was once a little girl who was given a lovely, bright red cloak by her grandmother. The little girl loved this cloak very much. She loved it so much in fact that she never wanted to take it off, and was always wearing it. Because of this, she became known as Little Red Riding Hood.

One sunny morning, Little Red Riding Hood's mother asked her if she would take some cakes and apple juice to her grandmother, who was ill.

Little Red Riding Hood loved her grandmother very much, and was pleased to be going to visit her.

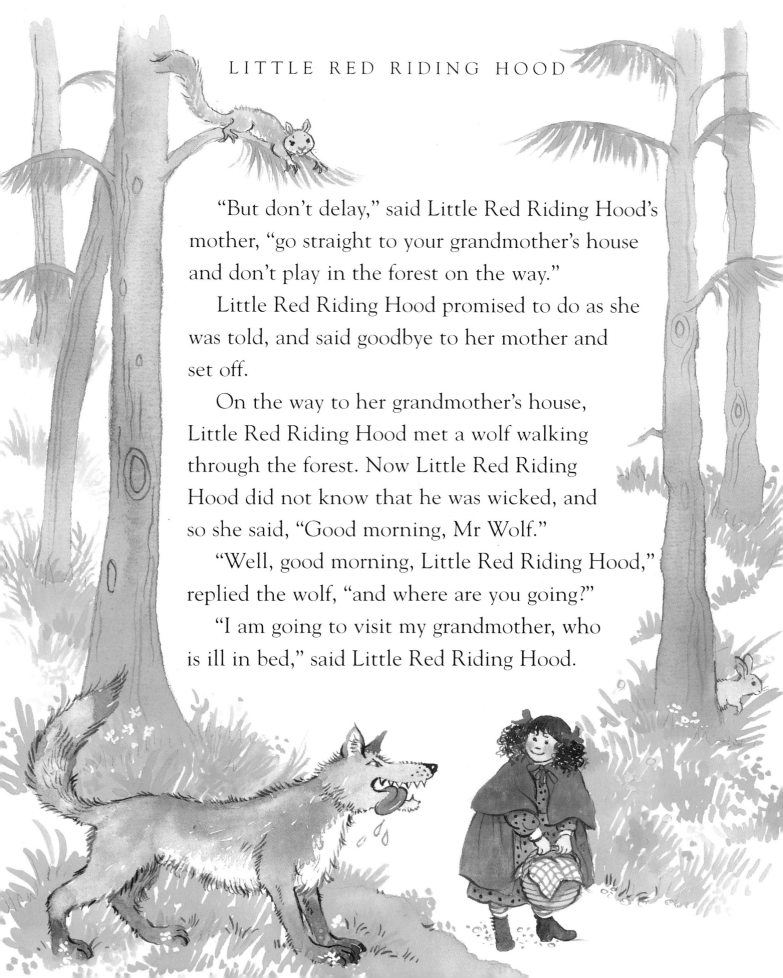

"But don't delay," said Little Red Riding Hood's mother, "go straight to your grandmother's house and don't play in the forest on the way."

Little Red Riding Hood promised to do as she was told, and said goodbye to her mother and set off.

On the way to her grandmother's house, Little Red Riding Hood met a wolf walking through the forest. Now Little Red Riding Hood did not know that he was wicked, and so she said, "Good morning, Mr Wolf."

"Well, good morning, Little Red Riding Hood," replied the wolf, "and where are you going?"

"I am going to visit my grandmother, who is ill in bed," said Little Red Riding Hood.

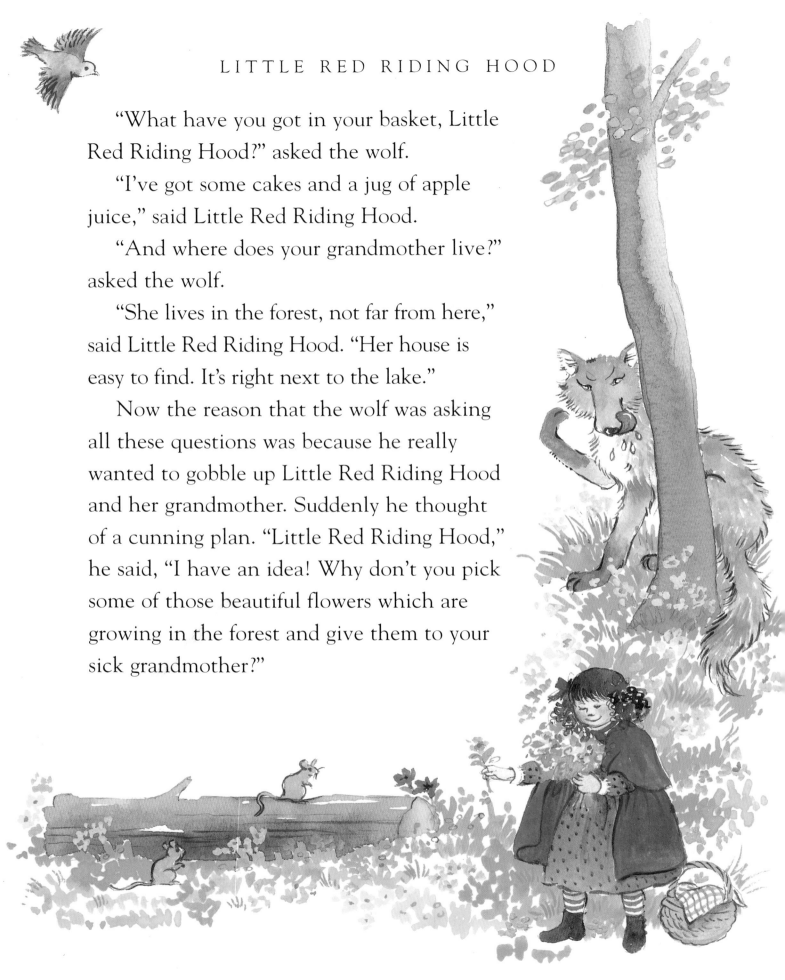

"What have you got in your basket, Little Red Riding Hood?" asked the wolf.

"I've got some cakes and a jug of apple juice," said Little Red Riding Hood.

"And where does your grandmother live?" asked the wolf.

"She lives in the forest, not far from here," said Little Red Riding Hood. "Her house is easy to find. It's right next to the lake."

Now the reason that the wolf was asking all these questions was because he really wanted to gobble up Little Red Riding Hood and her grandmother. Suddenly he thought of a cunning plan. "Little Red Riding Hood," he said, "I have an idea! Why don't you pick some of those beautiful flowers which are growing in the forest and give them to your sick grandmother?"

"What a good idea," said Little Red Riding Hood. "My grandmother would be so pleased to have some of these pretty flowers. I'm sure they would make her feel better."

And with that, she set about picking a big bunch of the prettiest flowers she could find. In fact, she was so busy looking for flowers that she didn't see the crafty wolf skip away and make off towards her grandmother's house. The wolf soon came to the house, and knocked on the door.

"Who is it?" said Grandmother.

"It's me, Little Red Riding Hood," said the wolf. "I've brought you some cakes and a jug of apple juice."

"Come in, come in, my dear," said Grandmother, "the door isn't locked."

The wolf then went into the house, and as soon as he saw the old lady lying in bed, he ran straight over to her and gobbled her up. Next he put on her nightdress and her frilly night cap and jumped into her bed, pulling the bed clothes up to his chin.

In a little while, Little Red Riding Hood – who had by now picked a lovely bunch of flowers for her grandmother – came hurrying up the garden path. The door to her grandmother's house was still open and so she went inside and walked over to the bed. Little Red Riding Hood could only see a little bit of her face poking out from the bed clothes.

"My, Grandmother, what big ears you have," said Little Red Riding Hood.

138

"All the better to hear you with, my dear," said the wolf.

"My, Grandmother, what big eyes you have," said Little Red Riding Hood.

"All the better to see you with, my dear," said the wolf.

"My, Grandmother, what big hands you have," said Little Red Riding Hood.

"All the better to hold you tight with, my dear," said the wolf.

"My, Grandmother, what big teeth you have," said Little Red Riding Hood.

"All the better to eat you with, my dear," cried the wolf. And with that he jumped out of bed and gobbled her up.

The wolf felt very full and rather sleepy after he had eaten Little Red Riding Hood. After all, he'd already just eaten her grandmother, too. So he went back to bed and fell asleep, snoring loudly.

Just then, a hunter was passing the house and heard the snoring. He looked through the window, and when he saw the wolf lying in bed, he realised that the wolf must have eaten the old lady. So, while the wolf was still sleeping, the hunter took his knife and cut open the wolf's stomach. To the hunter's great surprise, out popped Little Red Riding Hood and her grandmother. Luckily, the hunter had arrived just in time and both were still alive.

Little Red Riding Hood and her grandmother both thanked the hunter for saving them, and the hunter took the dead wolf's skin and went home.

Little Red Riding Hood's grandmother ate the cakes and drank the apple juice, and soon she was feeling much better. And Little Red Riding Hood? Well, she decided that she would never talk to a wolf again!

The Runaway Train

Once upon a time, there was a little kingdom in a far-off place. Although the people in the kingdom were ruled by a kindly king, the kingdom was mountainous and barren, and many of the folk were very poor.

Each month, there was a market. Market day was a very important day for all the villagers in the kingdom, just as it is for folk everywhere.

The market was held in a big, broad valley nestling among the snowy peaks, and people made their way to it from far and wide to sell their crops, or to buy new clothes or things for their homes.

People living up in the mountains would take the mountain passes and walk down into the valley. Those living a little further down the mountain would saddle up their donkeys and mules and ride to the market. But for people living at the bottom of the mountains, the best way to get to the market was to take the old steam train. The train ran from the bottom of the mountains all the way up to the top, and then down into the valley.

One day, a poor farmer who lived at the bottom of the mountains woke up and went to harvest the crops on his small farm. But the crop was poor. There was barely enough food to make a meal for his family and himself.

The poor farmer wondered what he could sell at the market, in order that his family and himself might have enough food to eat. He had no crops to sell, and he had already sold almost everything else he could spare. The only thing he had left to sell was his cockatoo.

The thought of selling his cockatoo filled him with great sadness. The cockatoo was a fine-looking bird, with colourful ivory, red and yellow feathers. Not only was it fine-looking, but it was thought by everyone to be a very clever bird, too. It seemed to understand whatever you said, and was a great favourite with all the family.

The farmer looked at his hungry family and then he looked at the cockatoo. The cockatoo looked back at the farmer as if it understood what the farmer was thinking.

"I must sell the cockatoo at the market," said the farmer finally. "We have no crops to eat, and we must buy food. There is nothing else we can sell to raise the money we need."

On the very next market day, the farmer climbed aboard the train for its journey up the mountains and down into the valley to the market. In his hand, he held a little metal cage, and sitting in the cage, looking very sad, was his beloved cockatoo.

The old train collected more people from the villages and then began its long, steep journey up the mountains. It chuffed and puffed, and puffed and chuffed, but then suddenly with a bang, a clang and a groan, it came to a halt. The boiler on the old train had exploded! Then, slowly, the train started to roll back down the mountain slope. The driver tried the brakes, but it was no use the old train just carried on rolling backwards, gathering speed all the time.

Everyone on board was very frightened, for there was nothing to stop the train hurtling all the way down the track and overturning at the bottom of the mountains.

Suddenly, the farmer had an idea. He lifted the cockatoo's cage close to his head and spoke to the cockatoo. "Fly down the mountain, as fast as you can, and raise the alarm!" he said. Then he opened the cockatoo's cage and released the bird.

Down the mountain the cockatoo flew as fast as its wings could take it. Straight to the railway station it went, and landed on the steps of the station master's office.

"Hello, what are you doing here?" said the station master, for he recognised the cockatoo by its bright, colourful feathers.

The cockatoo flew into the air and hovered in front of the station master, then it flew out of his office. Then it flew back into the office, flapped its wings in front of the station master and flew out again.

"Well, I do believe you want me to follow you," said the station master. So he went outside.

Suddenly something made the station master look up towards the mountain, and he saw the runaway train. "Quick!" he called to his station guards. "Bring some sand and follow me!" The station master and the guards quickly loaded sacks of sand. Then they threw it on to the track. Backwards and forwards they went with their sacks of sand, until a great mound of sand lay across the track, right in the path of the runaway train.

Suddenly the runaway train came into sight, clanking and rumbling helplessly down the track. Then it hit the heap of sand on the track and, amid more rumbling and grinding, it came to a safe halt.

Shaken, but safe, the passengers climbed out of the carriages. The station master explained what had happened and how the cockatoo had helped stop the runaway train.

"How could I ever have thought of selling you, my friend," said the farmer to his cockatoo. "From now on, we will always keep you safely."

All the villagers were so grateful to the farmer and his cockatoo, that they all gave some of their crops to help feed the farmer and his family until his own crops grew again.

The Jealous Caterpillar

One spring day a green caterpillar sat on a leaf. He watched a beautiful butterfly flutter past him on the breeze. "It's not fair. Here I am stuck on this boring leaf with nothing to do and nowhere to go while that lucky creature can fly across the world and see far-off lands," thought the caterpillar crossly. "And what's more," he continued to himself, "not only has that butterfly got wings with which to fly, but he's beautiful, too. Look at poor me. I'm just a dull green. No-one will notice me because I'm the same colour as the leaf." The caterpillar really did feel very sorry for himself, and rather jealous. "Go and enjoy yourself. Don't worry about me," he called spitefully to the butterfly.

But the butterfly hadn't heard a single word the caterpillar had been muttering, and soon he flew away. The caterpillar suddenly decided that he was going to be like the butterfly. "I'll learn how to fly and I'll paint myself lovely colours so that I look beautiful, too," he thought. He looked around for something to paint himself with but, of course, there was nothing at all on the leaf. Then he tried to fly. He launched himself from his leaf and tried to flap his tail, but all he did was land on the leaf below.

Along came a ladybird. "Aha!" thought the caterpillar. "Here's a beautiful creature who knows how to fly. I'll ask her to teach me." So the caterpillar said, "Hello, I've been admiring your beautiful wingcase. Could you tell me how I, too, could be beautiful? And can you teach me to fly?"

The ladybird looked at the caterpillar. "Be patient and wait a while," she said wisely, "and soon enough you'll get what you want." And with that the ladybird went on her way.

"Whatever can she mean? She's just too proud to teach me," the caterpillar thought jealously.

Some time later a bee buzzed past and landed on a nearby leaf. "Aha!" thought the caterpillar. "Here's a beautiful creature who knows how to fly. I'll ask him to teach me." So the caterpillar said, "Hello, I've been admiring your beautiful striped back. Could you tell me how I, too, could be beautiful? And can you teach me to fly?"

The bee looked at the caterpillar. "You'll find out soon enough, young man," said the bee sternly. And with that he went on his way.

"Whatever can he mean? He's just too haughty to teach me," the caterpillar thought jealously.

Now a while later along came a bird. "Aha!" thought the caterpillar once more. "Here's a beautiful creature who knows how to fly. I'll ask him to teach me." So once again the caterpillar said, "Hello, I've been admiring your beautiful feathers. Could you tell me how I, too, could be beautiful? And can you teach me to fly?"

The bird looked at the caterpillar and thought to himself slyly that here was a very silly caterpillar, but he would make a tasty snack for his chicks. "Let's see if I can trick him," he thought.

"I can't give you wings and I can't make you beautiful. But I can show you the world. I expect you'd like to see the world, wouldn't you, little caterpillar?" said the bird.

"Oh, yes!" said the caterpillar in great excitement.

"Climb upon my back then, little caterpillar!" said the crafty bird.

151

The caterpillar did as he was told and the bird flew off towards his nest. At first the caterpillar clung tightly to the bird's back but soon he felt quite sleepy and eventually he dozed off and slipped from the bird's back. Down he fell through the air and landed on a leaf, but still he didn't wake up. Soon he was wrapped in a soft, brown, papery cocoon from which he would not wake up for a long while.

Meanwhile, the bird reached his nest. "Look at the treat I've brought you," he said to his chicks.

They looked very puzzled. "What treat, Dad?" one of them piped up.

"This nice juicy caterpillar," said the bird, shaking the feathers on his back. "Climb down, little caterpillar," he said. But of course there was nothing there. Now it was the father's turn to look puzzled, while the chicks laughed at him.

152

"Well, I must have dropped him," he said. "I've never done that before," he added. He flew out of the nest in search of the caterpillar but he was nowhere to be seen. Once he saw a strange brown, papery parcel on a leaf, but in the end the bird had to return to the nest with his beak empty.

A long while later the caterpillar woke up. "I must get out of this stuffy wrapping," he thought, as he pushed his way out.

He stood on the leaf and yawned and stretched. As he stretched, he noticed to his amazement two pairs of beautiful wings spreading out on either side of his body. "Are they really mine?" he wondered. He tried lifting and turning them and yes, he could make them work. He looked at his reflection in a raindrop and saw a lovely butterfly staring back at him. "So the ladybird and the bee were right," he exclaimed. "How foolish I was to be a jealous caterpillar," he declared to a passing ant, "for now I am a beautiful butterfly after all."

The Enchanted Harp

Long ago there lived a pedlar. Every day he took up the same place in the market square with his harp. Now this was no ordinary harp. It was an enchanted harp. The pedlar would call out to passers-by and, for a penny, the harp would play all on its own any tune they wished. It could play any sort of tune from the slowest, most tearful ballad to the liveliest, happiest jig. It could play music for any occasion. Sometimes a wedding party would come by just to have the harp play a tune for the bride and groom.

Now one day a young man passed through the town. He heard the sound of the harp's sweet music coming from the market square and made his way over to where the pedlar stood. He couldn't believe his eyes or his ears! The harp was playing a lullaby for a lady with a baby that was crying. The music was so enchanting that the baby soon stopped wailing and was fast asleep. Then he saw an old man give the pedlar a penny and whisper in his ear. The harp changed its tune and now it played an ancient melody that the old man had not heard for many a year, and his eyes filled with tears of gratitude.

The young man watched all this and thought to himself, "If only that harp were mine. I could make a lot more money with it than that silly old pedlar!" He waited a while for the crowd to disperse, and then when he thought no-one was looking he went up to the pedlar and said, "People say that on this day a great spotted pig will fall out of the sky and land on the market square.

Keep a look out and if you see a pair of trotters in the sky, get out of the way fast!" And he pointed up at the sky. The pedlar peered upwards but all he could see were scudding white clouds. While he was staring up, the young man snatched the harp and was out of the market square and away down the street before the pedlar realised what had happened.

"Stop! Thief!" the pedlar shouted. But it was too late. By the time folk gave chase the young man had gone. He didn't stop running until he reached a town many miles away, where no-one had seen the enchanted harp before.

The young man set up the harp and called out to passers-by, "Two pennies and my harp will play any tune you wish!" A man and woman came up and asked for a waltz and, sure enough, the harp began to play. The couple spun round the square merrily and were happy enough to give the young man two pennies.

More and more people came by and asked for tunes. The young man rubbed his hands with pleasure. "I shall surely make my fortune now," he said to himself.

Weeks passed and the young man did, indeed, make a lot of money. He didn't care at all how much he charged. If someone who looked wealthy came along he might charge them six pennies or even eight. By now he had completely forgotten that he had stolen the harp and that it didn't belong to him at all. He bought himself fine clothes and ate expensive food and generally considered himself rather clever.

Then one day an old man in a broad-brimmed hat came past and asked for a tune. He grumbled a bit when the young man asked for two pennies but held out the coins, making sure the young man could not see his face – for he was the pedlar!

"I'd like the harp to play a tune to drive you mad," said the old man. The young man thought this was a strange request but he had taken the coins and the harp had already started to play.

It played a short and very silly tune. Then it played it again. And again. And again. And again. It simply wouldn't stop. By now the old man had slipped away, so when people weren't watching the young man tried to kick the harp, but it side-stepped him and carried on playing. On and on it went, playing that infuriating tune. The young man put his hands over his ears to block out the noise, but the harp just played louder.

Passers-by moved away. "What a terrible tune," they said. The young man tried to move away, too, but the harp just followed him down the road, still playing.

Everywhere he went, night and day, the harp followed the young man until he was at his wits' end. He had used up all his money and he was in despair. Finally, he thought there was only one thing to do. He must go back to the pedlar and beg him to stop the harp. It took him a while to make his way back to the town where the pedlar lived, but sure enough there he was, standing in the market square trying to sell a few old pots and pans to passers-by. He looked very unhappy, and the young man felt truly sorry for what he had done.

He approached the pedlar with the harp still playing away behind him. He was about to explain when, to his surprise, the pedlar stopped him and said, "I know all about your plight. I will stop the harp playing its maddening tune on one condition."

"I'll do anything," said the young man.

"You must ask people what tune they would liked played and then you must give them a penny each time."

The young man gratefully agreed and the pedlar told the harp to stop playing. The young man had to work very hard to earn enough money to give people their pennies, but he was willing to do so in return for the pedlar making the harp stop playing that maddening tune!

Puss in Boots

Once upon a time in France, there lived a miller who had three sons. When he died, the miller left the mill to his eldest son. To his second son he left a donkey on whose back sacks of flour could be loaded and delivered to customers. But to the youngest son, who was much the most handsome of the three, he left only a large cat, whose job it had been to chase the mice that came at night to make holes in the sacks and steal grain.

The poor youngest brother wondered how on earth he would make his living with only the cat for company. He could see that he would have to go out into the world to seek his fortune. "I shall have to leave you behind, Puss," he said, "for I don't see how I am to look after you."

"What about if I looked after *you?*" replied Puss.

"Whatever do you mean?" said his master.

"I can make your fortune for you," said the cat. "All I need is a good – sized drawstring bag and a pair of really nice boots – for my hind feet."

Well, the lad was mightily puzzled, but he decided it was worth letting the cat try to win his fortune, as he surely had no idea of what to do otherwise. With his brand new boots on his hind paws and his drawstring bag slung over his shoulder, Puss set off with nothing but a handful of corn from the mill.

The first thing he did was go straight to the nearest rabbit warren where he opened the bag, put a little corn into it and laid it open near the rabbit hole. Then Puss laid in wait until dusk, when the rabbits came out of their hole. One rabbit came up, full of curiosity, and hopped into the bag to get the corn. Up sprang Puss and pulled the drawstring tight. Then, instead of taking the rabbit to his master, he set off to the palace, where he announced that he had brought the king a present.

"Your majesty," said Puss, taking a low bow, "I am a messenger from the Marquis of Carabas, your neighbour. He was out hunting today and was lucky enough to catch a fine young rabbit. He begs that you will accept it as a present."

The king was puzzled, because he'd never heard of this Marquis, but he was pleased to have the rabbit. "Tell your master that I am delighted with his kind present," he said.

Day after day, Puss went out hunting in this manner and each time he presented his catch to the king. "Don't forget," he said to his master, "that you're supposed to be a Marquis." The young boy had no idea what the cat was talking about, but he trusted him nevertheless. After a while the cat started to be invited in for a drink and a chat with the guards and he soon got to know all the court gossip. One time, Puss got to hear that the king was planning to drive the next day in his grand carriage with his daughter, the most beautiful princess in France. Puss took care to find out which direction they intended to take.

The next morning he said to his master, "I think it would be a good idea to take a swim in the river this morning." The lad agreed and, by the look in Puss's eye, he knew that he had a plan in mind. Puss led the way to a part of the river where the royal carriage was bound to pass. While the boy was swimming in the river, Puss heard the sound of the approaching carriage. Quickly Puss hid his master's ragged clothes under a stone and as the carriage came into view he ran into the road shouting, "Help! The Marquis of Carabas is drowning!" At once the king recognised Puss and ordered his guards to go to the rescue. The lad pretended to be drowning, so that the guards had quite a struggle to get him to the bank.

Meanwhile, Puss went up to the carriage, bowed to the king and said, "While he was bathing, thieves unfortunately stole my master's fine clothing. He cannot appear before your daughter without any clothes."

"Of course not," replied the king, and sent his footman to fetch a spare set of clothes from the back of the royal carriage. Now that the handsome lad was properly dressed, the king was glad to meet the mysterious Marquis, of whom he had heard so much from Puss. He welcomed the 'Marquis' into the carriage, where he sat next to the princess. "Come for a drive with us, my dear Marquis," said the king.

Without another word Puss set off and disappeared around the next bend of the road. By the time the king's gilded carriage was on its way again, Puss was a long way ahead. Soon he passed a field of haymakers. "My good haymakers," said Puss, "you must tell the king that this meadow belongs to the Marquis of Carabas – or I'll grind you all to little pieces."

Now Puss knew that the meadow really belonged to an ogre, who was known to be able to change his shape. So of course the haymakers had no idea if this was just an ordinary pussy cat telling them what to do – or if it really was the ogre. Soon the royal carriage passed by and the king leaned out and asked to whom the field belonged. "To the Marquis of Carabas, your majesty," chorused the haymakers.

"That's a fine piece of land you've got there," said the king, nudging the lad who was busy chatting to the princess.

All along the road it was the same story. Puss always got there before the royal carriage. Woodcutters, shepherds, and farmers all told the king that their master was the Marquis of Carabas, because Puss had threatened to turn them all into mincemeat if they didn't. Now Puss caught sight of a fine castle which he recognised as belonging to the ogre.

Puss went up to the great gate and asked to speak to the ogre. Puss said to him, "I heard that you can transform yourself in the most amazing way – into a lion for example. But I really can't believe that this is true."

The ogre was so offended that he bellowed, "JUST YOU WATCH!" and instantly turned himself into a lion. Puss pretended to be scared and jumped up on to the castle roof. The ogre turned himself back into an ogre. "That'll teach you," he roared.

"You gave me a dreadful fright," said Puss. "Do you know, people say you can even turn yourself into a tiny animal, such as rat or mouse. But that's absurd. It's quite impossible."

"IMPOSSIBLE, EH?" screeched the ogre, and the great foolish creature turned himself into a mouse.

In an instant, Puss had pounced on him and gobbled him up, bones and all. At that moment, the royal carriage rumbled over the drawbridge, for the king, too, had spotted the castle and wondered who lived there.

166

"Welcome to the castle of the Marquis of Carabas, your majesty," said Puss, who had just wiped the last morsels of the ogre from his whiskers.

"What," cried the king, turning to the young boy, "is this yours, too?" The lad glanced at Puss and then nodded. "May we see inside?" went on the king.

So the king, the princess and the miller's son looked around the castle. And very fine it was, too. The ogre's servants were so happy to see the back of their master that they laid on a fine feast. And at the end of the meal, the king agreed to give his daughter's hand in marriage to the 'Marquis'.

As for Puss, his master was so grateful that he saw to it that the cat was made a lord. So they all lived happily ever after and Puss never had to chase another mouse for the rest of his life.

Bobby's Best Birthday Present

It was the morning of Bobby's birthday and he was very excited. When he came down to breakfast, there on the table was a big pile of presents. Bobby opened them one by one. There was a beautiful book with pictures of wild animals, a toy racing car and a baseball cap. Bobby was very pleased with his presents, but where was the present from his parents? "Close your eyes and hold out your hands!" said his mother. When he opened his eyes there was a large rectangular parcel in his hands. Bobby tore off the wrapping and inside was a box. And inside the box was a wonderful, shiny, electric train set.

For a moment, Bobby looked at the train set lying in the box. It was so lovely he could hardly bear to touch it. There was an engine and six carriages all lying neatly on their sides. Bobby carefully lifted the engine out of the box. Then he set up the track and soon he had the train whizzing round his bedroom floor. Freddie the cat came in and watched the train going round. Round and round she watched it go, then one time when the train came past her she swiped at it with her paw and derailed it. The engine and the six carriages came tumbling off the track and landed in a heap on the floor. "Look what you've done!" wailed Bobby as he picked up the train and reassembled it. The carriages were undamaged, but the engine had hit the side of his bed and was badly dented.

Bobby was very upset. "My brand new train is ruined!" he cried.

"Don't worry, Bobby," said his mother, "we can't take it back to the shop now, but we can take it to the toymender in the morning. I'm sure he'll make a good job of mending the engine and it'll look as good as new again." Bobby played with his racing car, he wore his new baseball cap and he read his new book, but really all he wanted to do was to play with his train set. He went to bed that night with the engine on the floor near his bed.

In the morning when Bobby woke up, the first thing he did was to look at the poor broken engine of his train set. He picked it up, expecting to see the buckled metal, but the engine was perfect. He couldn't believe his eyes! He ran to his parents. "Look, look!" he cried. They were as amazed as he was. The engine worked perfectly and Bobby played happily with his train set all day – but he made sure Freddie kept out of his room!

That night Bobby couldn't sleep. He lay in bed tossing and turning. Then he heard a noise. It was the sound of his train set rushing round the track. He peered into the darkness and yes, he could definitely make out the shape of the train as it sped by. How had the train started? It couldn't start all by itself! Had Freddie crept into his room and flicked the switch? As his eyes gradually became accustomed to the dark Bobby could make out several shapes in the carriages. Who were the mysterious passengers? He slid out of bed and on to the floor beside the train set. Now he could see that the passengers were little folk wearing strange pointed hats and leafy costumes. "Elves!" thought Bobby.

At that moment one of the elves spotted Bobby. "Hello there!" he called as the train rushed past again. "We saw that your train set was broken. We so much wanted a ride that we fixed it. I hope you don't mind!" Bobby was too astounded to say anything at all. "Come with us for a ride," called the elf as his carriage approached again.

As the train passed him the elf leaned out of the carriage and grabbed Bobby by the hand. Bobby felt himself shrinking as he flew through the air, and the next instant he was sitting beside the elf in the carriage of his very own train set! "Here we go – hold tight!" called the elf as the train left the track and went out through the window into the night sky.

"Now, where would you like to go? What would you like to see?" asked the elf.

"Toyland!" replied Bobby without hesitation. Sure enough, the train headed towards a track which curved up a mountain made of pink and white sugar. Beside the track were toys going about their daily business. Bobby saw a ragdoll getting into a shiny tin car. Then a wooden sailor puppet wound up the car with a large key and off went the doll. He saw three teddy bears setting off for school with their satchels on their backs. Then he saw a brightly coloured clown playing a drum.

The train stopped and Bobby and the elves got out. "Now for some fun!" said one of the elves. They had come to a halt by a toy fairground. Bobby found that this was like no other fairground he had ever been to before. For in Toyland, all the rides are real. The horses on the carousel were real horses. The dodgem cars were real cars. And when he got in the rocket for the rocket ride, it took him all the way to the moon and back!

"Time to go, Bobby," said one of the elves at last. "It'll be morning soon." Bobby climbed wearily back into the train and soon he was fast asleep. When he woke up it was morning, and he was back in his bed. The train set lay quite still on its tracks. But in one of the carriages was a scrap of paper and on the paper, in tiny spidery writing, were the words: *We hope you enjoyed your trip to Toyland – the elves.*

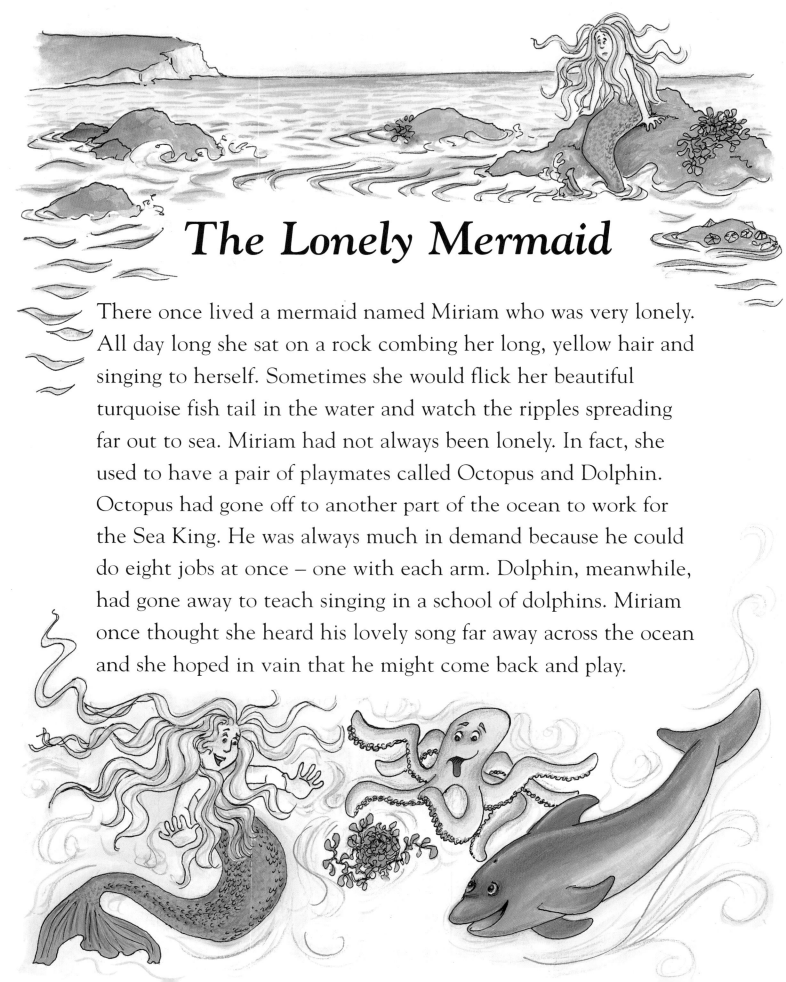

The Lonely Mermaid

There once lived a mermaid named Miriam who was very lonely.
All day long she sat on a rock combing her long, yellow hair and
singing to herself. Sometimes she would flick her beautiful
turquoise fish tail in the water and watch the ripples spreading
far out to sea. Miriam had not always been lonely. In fact, she
used to have a pair of playmates called Octopus and Dolphin.
Octopus had gone off to another part of the ocean to work for
the Sea King. He was always much in demand because he could
do eight jobs at once – one with each arm. Dolphin, meanwhile,
had gone away to teach singing in a school of dolphins. Miriam
once thought she heard his lovely song far away across the ocean
and she hoped in vain that he might come back and play.

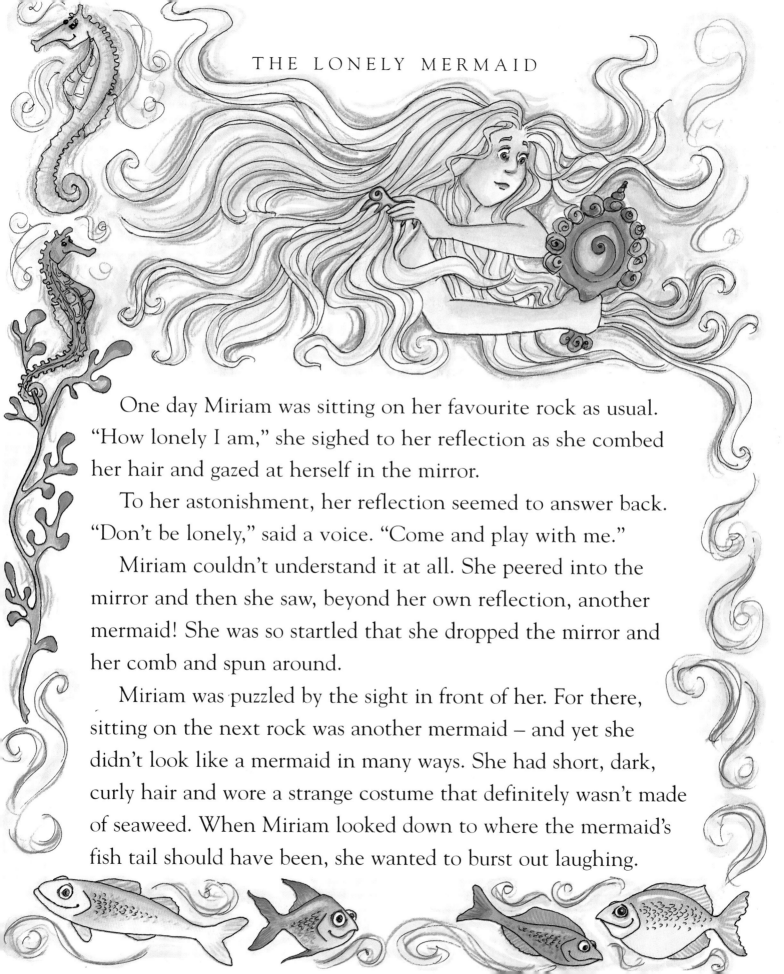

One day Miriam was sitting on her favourite rock as usual. "How lonely I am," she sighed to her reflection as she combed her hair and gazed at herself in the mirror.

To her astonishment, her reflection seemed to answer back. "Don't be lonely," said a voice. "Come and play with me."

Miriam couldn't understand it at all. She peered into the mirror and then she saw, beyond her own reflection, another mermaid! She was so startled that she dropped the mirror and her comb and spun around.

Miriam was puzzled by the sight in front of her. For there, sitting on the next rock was another mermaid – and yet she didn't look like a mermaid in many ways. She had short, dark, curly hair and wore a strange costume that definitely wasn't made of seaweed. When Miriam looked down to where the mermaid's fish tail should have been, she wanted to burst out laughing.

For instead of a beautiful tail, the other mermaid had two strange limbs like an extra long pair of arms stretching down.

The other 'mermaid', who was really a little girl called Georgie, was equally amazed by the sight of Miriam. She had seen pictures of mermaids in books before, but now she couldn't quite believe her eyes. For here, on the rock beside her, was a real live mermaid!

For a moment they were both too astonished to speak. Then they both said at once, "Who are you?"

"I'm Miriam," said Miriam.

"I'm Georgie," said Georgie.

"Let's go for a swim," said Miriam. Soon the two of them were in the water, chasing each other and giggling.

"Let's play tag along the beach," suggested Georgie, and started swimming towards the shore. She had quite forgotten that Miriam would not be able to run around on dry land. Miriam followed though she was rather afraid, as her mother had always told her not to go near the shore in case she got stranded. Georgie ran out of the water and up on to the beach.

"Wait for me!" called Miriam, struggling in the water as her tail thrashed about. Then, to her astonishment, something strange happened. She found she could leave the water with ease and, looking down, saw that her tail had disappeared and that in its place were two of those strange long arm things like Georgie's.

176

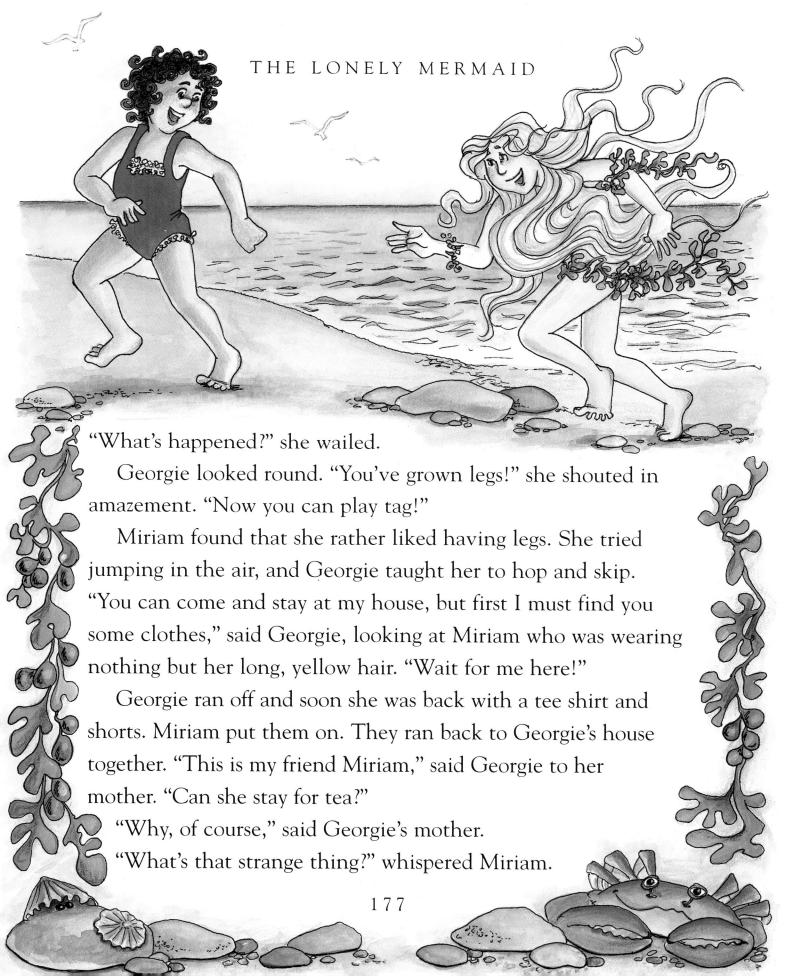

"What's happened?" she wailed.

Georgie looked round. "You've grown legs!" she shouted in amazement. "Now you can play tag!"

Miriam found that she rather liked having legs. She tried jumping in the air, and Georgie taught her to hop and skip. "You can come and stay at my house, but first I must find you some clothes," said Georgie, looking at Miriam who was wearing nothing but her long, yellow hair. "Wait for me here!"

Georgie ran off and soon she was back with a tee shirt and shorts. Miriam put them on. They ran back to Georgie's house together. "This is my friend Miriam," said Georgie to her mother. "Can she stay for tea?"

"Why, of course," said Georgie's mother.

"What's that strange thing?" whispered Miriam.

"It's a chair," said Georgie. She showed Miriam how to sit on the chair. All through teatime Miriam watched Georgie to see how she should eat from a plate and drink from a cup and saucer. She'd never tasted food like this before. How she wished she could have chocolate cake at home under the sea!

After tea Miriam said, "Now I'll show *you* how to do something." Taking Georgie by the hand she led her down to the beach again. There they picked up shells, and then Miriam showed Georgie how to make a lovely necklace from shells threaded with seaweed. While they made their necklaces, Miriam taught Georgie how to sing songs of the sea.

Soon it was bedtime. "You can sleep in the spare bed in my room," said Georgie. Miriam slipped in between the sheets. How strange it felt! She was used to feeling water all around her and here she was lying in a bed. She tossed and turned, feeling hotter and hotter, and couldn't sleep at all. In the middle of the night she got up and threw open the window to get some fresh air.

She could smell the salty sea air and she began to feel rather homesick. Then she heard a familiar sound from far away. It was Dolphin calling to her! The noise was getting closer and closer until at last Miriam knew what she must do. She slipped out of the house and ran down to the beach in the moonlight. As soon as her toes touched the water, her legs turned back into a fish tail and she swam out to sea to join Dolphin.

The next morning, when Georgie woke up, she was very upset to find that her friend had gone. When she told her mother who Miriam really was, her mother said, "The sea is a mermaid's true home and that's where she belongs. But I'm sure you two will always be friends."

And indeed, from time to time, Georgie was sure that she could see Miriam waving to her from the sea.

The Red Daffodil

It was spring time and all the daffodils were pushing their heads up towards the warmth of the sun. Slowly, their golden petals unfolded to let their yellow trumpets dance in the breeze. One particular field of daffodils was a blaze of gold like all the others – but right in the middle was a single splash of red. For there in the middle was a red daffodil.

From the moment she opened her petals, the red daffodil knew she was different from the other flowers. They sneered at her and whispered to each other. "What a strange, poor creature!" said one.

"She must envy our beautiful golden colour," said another.

And indeed it was true. The red daffodil wished very much that she was like the others. Instead of being proud of her red petals, she was ashamed and hung her head low. "What's wrong with me?" she thought. "Why aren't there any other red daffodils in the field?"

Passers-by stopped to admire the field of beautiful daffodils. "What a wonderful sight!" they exclaimed. And the daffodils' heads swelled with pride and danced in the breeze all the more merrily.

Then someone spotted the red daffodil right in the middle of the field. "Look at that extraordinary flower!" the man shouted. Everyone peered into the centre of the field.

"You're right," said someone else, "there's a red daffodil in the middle." Soon a large crowd had gathered, all pointing and laughing at the red daffodil.

She could feel herself blushing even redder at the attention. "How I wish my petals would close up again," she said to herself in anguish. But try as she might, her fine red trumpet stood out for all to see.

Now, in the crowd of people gathered at the edge of the field was a little girl. People were pushing and shoving and she couldn't see anything at all. At last, her father lifted her high upon his shoulders so that she could see into the field. "Oh!" exclaimed the little girl in a very big voice. "So that's the red daffodil. I think it's really beautiful. What a lucky daffodil to be so different."

And do you know, other people heard what the little girl said and they began to whisper to each other, "Well, I must say, I actually thought myself it was rather pretty, you know." Before long, people were praising the daffodil's beauty and saying it must be a very special flower. The red daffodil heard what the crowd was saying. Now she was blushing with pride and held her head as high as all the other daffodils in the field.

The other daffodils were furious. "What a foolish crowd," said one indignantly. "We are the beautiful ones!" They turned their heads away from the red daffodil and ignored her. She began to feel unhappy again.

By now word had spread far and wide about the amazing red daffodil and people came from all over the land to see her. Soon, the king's daughter got to hear about the red daffodil. "I must see this for myself," said the princess. She set off with her servant and eventually they came to the field where the red daffodil grew. When the princess saw her, she clapped her hands with glee.

"The red daffodil is more beautiful than I ever imagined," she cried. Then she had an idea. "Please bring my pet dove," she said to her servant. The man looked rather puzzled, but soon he returned with the bird. "As you know," said the princess to the servant, "I am to be married tomorrow and I would dearly love to have that red daffodil in my wedding bouquet."

The princess sent the dove into the middle of the field and it gently picked up the daffodil in its beak and brought her back to where the princess stood. The princess carried the daffodil back to the palace. She put the daffodil in a vase of water and there she stayed until the next day.

In the morning, the princess's servant took the red daffodil to the church. She could hear the bells and see all the guests assembling for the wedding ceremony. Then she saw the princess arrive in a coach driven by four white horses. How lovely the princess looked in her white gown and her head crowned with deep red roses.

As the servant reached the church door, the princess's lady-in-waiting stepped forward holding a huge bouquet of flowers into which she placed the red daffodil just as the flowers were handed to the princess. For a while, the red daffodil was overcome by the powerful scents of the other flowers in the bouquet, but when at last she looked around her she realised, with astonishment, that all of them were red. There were red daisies, red lilies, red carnations and red foxgloves. "Welcome," said one of the daisies, "you're one of us." And for the first time in her life, the red daffodil felt really at home.

After the wedding, the princess scattered the flowers from her bouquet among the flowers in her garden. Every spring, when she opened her petals, the red daffodil found she was surrounded by lots of other red flowers, and she lived happily in the garden for many, many years.

Morag the Witch

Morag was just an ordinary witch – until the day she enrolled for a course of advanced spell casting at the Wizard, Witch and Warlock Institute of Magic. For that was where she met Professor Fizzlestick. Now Professor Fizzlestick was a very wise old man indeed. Morag, on the other hand, was a very vain young witch who didn't know as much as she thought she did. She could turn people into frogs if they really deserved it, and do other simple spells like that, but she still had a lot to learn. The problem was, Morag thought she was the most perfect little witch in the whole wide world.

Morag's adventure started on her very first day at school. At the beginning of the day, after all the young witches and wizards had made friends and met the teachers, they were called in one by one to talk to Professor Fizzlestick.

"Now, young Morag Bendlebaum, I taught both your mother and your father," said the professor in a very serious voice, "and a very fine witch and wizard they turned out to be, too. So, what kind of witch do you think you are going to be?"

Without giving this any thought at all, Morag blurted out, "I'm better than my parents, and I'm probably better than you!"

This answer surprised even Morag, for although she thought this was true, she didn't actually mean to say it.

"Don't be surprised by your answers," said Professor Fizzlestick, "there is a truth spell in this room, and whatever you truly believe you must say. And I have to say that you appear to have an enormously high opinion of yourself. Why don't you tell me what makes you so very good?"

"I'm clever," said Morag, "and I'm good, and I'm always right."

"But what about your dark side?" said Professor Fizzlestick.

"I'm sorry to disappoint you," replied Morag quite seriously, "but I'm afraid I simply don't have a dark side."

187

"Well in that case I would like you to meet someone very close to you," said Professor Fizzlestick with a smile on his lips.

Morag looked over to where Professor Fizzlestick pointed, and was startled to see on the sofa next to her... herself!

As Morag stared open-mouthed with astonishment, the professor explained that if, as she believed, she was without a dark side, then there was absolutely nothing to worry about. "If, however," he continued, "you have deceived yourself, then I'm afraid you are in for a few surprises."

With that the professor dismissed them both from the room and told them to get to know each other. As Morag and her dark side stood outside the professor's room, Morag's dark side jumped and whooped for joy. "At last," she cried, "I'm free. I don't have to sit and listen to you telling me what's right all day; I don't have to keep persuading you to choose the biggest slice of cake before your brother – in fact, I don't, I repeat **don't,** have to do anything that you tell me at all."

So saying she broke into a run and rushed down the corridor, knocking over chairs and bumping into other little witches and wizards along the way. Morag was horrified. She would have to follow her dark side and stop her from causing trouble. Morag chased after her dark side and finally caught up with her at the chocolate machine. "Don't eat all that chocolate," cried Morag. "You know it's bad for your teeth and will ruin your appetite for lunch!"

"Tsk!" scoffed her dark side. "You might not want any chocolate but I certainly do!" And with that she ran off once more, dropping chocolate on to the freshly polished floor as well as pushing a big piece into her mouth.

Just then, the bell sounded for lunch. Although Morag felt she ought to find her dark side, she also knew that the bell was a command to go to the dining hall, and she mustn't disobey it. Morag sat down to lunch next to her friend, Topaz. She was just about to tell her what had happened, when she saw that Topaz was not eating her vegetables! Morag scolded Topaz for this, and gave her a lecture on eating healthily.

Topaz stared at Morag in amazement, then peered closely at her. "What's happened to you?" she asked.

Morag explained what had happened in Professor Fizzlestick's office, and then declared, "And you know, it's the best thing that has ever happened to me. I thought I was good before, but now I'm even better. I never want my dark side back again, but we must find her and lock her up so that she can do no harm."

Topaz agreed that they must find her dark side, but secretly hoped that she and Morag would be re-united. Morag wasn't Morag without her dark side.

After lunch, Morag went for her first lesson of the afternoon. When she walked into the classroom she discovered her dark side already there, busy preparing spells! Morag's dark side had already prepared a 'turning a nose into an elephant's trunk' spell and a 'turning skin into dragons' scales' spell and was just finishing off a 'turning your teacher into stone' spell!

Morag suddenly heard a trumpeting noise from the back of the classroom. She turned to find that the wizard twins, Denzil and Dorian Dillydally, had both sprouted huge grey trunks down to the ground where their noses had been. Morag rushed over to her dark side to make her change them back, but before she could reach her she tripped over a creature crouching down on the floor. It looked just like a dragon and it was wearing a purple and white spotted dress last seen on Betina Bumblebag. Morag's dark side was casting spells all over the place. "Oh, why doesn't the teacher stop her!" cried Morag to Topaz.

I'm sure you've guessed by now. Nice Miss Chuckle was entirely turned to stone from head to foot!

Just then Professor Fizzlestick walked into the classroom. Morag pointed to her dark side, still making spells at the front of the classroom.

190

"Lock her up immediately," Morag begged the professor.

"I'm afraid that you are the only one who can do that," said the wise old man. "The two of you are inseparable and you need each other. Without your dark side you would be unbearable and without you she is dreadful. Have I your permission to lock her back inside you?"

Even though Morag didn't want any part of her dark side back, she agreed reluctantly. Her dark side instantly disappeared, and Morag felt... wonderful! Oh, it was so good to be back to normal, to be basically good, but occasionally mischievous.

"Thank you," said Morag to the professor. "I think I've learned something very valuable today."

"There is good and bad in everyone," replied the professor, "even the most perfect of witches."

Morag blushed when she remembered what she had said earlier that morning, but she was so relieved to find she was normal that she really didn't mind. Morag and Topaz went back to the classroom to undo all the bad things Morag's dark side had done, but on the way they both felt a huge urge for a snack, so they stopped at the chocolate machine first!